Christmas Is

DOOMED

VICKI SWEETS

ISBN: 979-8-9895335-1-0

For those who wanted all those cute Christmas
rom-coms to be a tiny bit spicier… this one's for you!

Christmas Is

DOOMED

ONE

Nothing is going to spoil today.

The air is crisp, fresh snow will soon fall, and my house smells like cinnamon. I turn up the Christmas music, twirling in my red dress that falls just below my stocking-covered knees. My copper hair is perfectly curled, and I let it fall over my shoulders in thick, loose spirals.

Nothing at all will spoil this day. Especially with my music drowning out what's happening outside.

Coffee is a must, with cream and vanilla. Breakfast is potatoes with veggies and cheese. Shoes are my favorite black boots because I still believe they go with everything.

Nothing will go wrong. Nothing at all.

He will not spoil my day.

My day is wrapped in an impenetrable forcefield of Christmas joy and winter cheer.

Two bedrooms, two bathrooms, a small living room, and a kitchen with space for a breakfast nook. I stride through them all, admiring my safe haven. My purse sits discarded behind the Christmas tree that's centered in the large, front window. I climb over a pile of broken string lights, and I snatch my purse from the ground, slinging it over my shoulder.

My living room looks like Santa's elves took over. Candy canes and cute characters cover every surface. Papier-mâché snowmen and snowflakes hang from my ceiling, and cozy blankets are nestled neatly against pillows.

It's what Christmas should look like.

And not at all like what's happening outside.

I glance at the old grandfather clock near the hallway, smiling at my perfect timing. If there's no distractions, I can take a leisurely drive to work.

It's the perfect morning, dammit, and nothing and no one will ruin it.

I shove my arms into my jacket, throw a scarf around my shoulders, and open my door. Shutting my eyes, I take a deep breath of winter air.

Fresh. Frozen.

Exquisite.

Perfection.

"Incoming!"

Slam!

"You," I seethe in a dark, loathsome growl, my holiday spirit forgotten as the slushy remains of a snowball slumps from the side of my house. It made contact less than two feet from my head. It could have pulverized me!

I drop my gaze, glaring at the mess it makes on my tidy front porch.

"Hiya, Red!" His voice is annoyingly familiar and devastatingly deep.

God, why does he have to sound like that?

"You having a good morning?"

Grudgingly, I lift my gaze to the man across the street. The crease between my brows is starting to feel rather permanent as I frown for the umpteenth time in his direction.

God, why does he have to look like that?

Theo Kase. My neighbor. New to town as of February this year. Food enthusiast, gym rat (I assume, based on his physique), and good Samaritan in the eyes of everyone in town.

Also, my nemesis.

The devil incarnate.

"Mr. Kase," I state in greeting, taking a large step forward.

He smiles and looks at me like he's ready to wrestle. He's been pushing me closer and closer to the metaphorical edge, and he looks like he's hoping the snowball will be the final straw. He steps into the street, rubbing his hands together and smirking as he appraises me.

I take the three steps down from my porch and walk briskly forward, pleased with myself for shoveling my walkway and clearing my steps before the sun was fully up.

"As I've asked before," I start, walking towards my truck and tugging the hem of my jacket sleeves down. "I prefer you don't *gift me* with anymore of your creative nicknames."

"Ah, but Red fits you," he taunts.

Behind him, giant inflatables fill his yard and holiday pop music floats through the air. But it's the bad sort of holiday pop music. The worst kind, actually. There's nothing classic or good about it. There's a reindeer sliding down a pole on one side of his yard, and there's an elf looking in a shed while its butt crack sticks out. His yard is crude, and the neighbors should hate it, but the kids laugh, and the adults shake their heads with smiles.

I want to ignore it, but it's right in my face, casting a dark cloud over my realistic reindeer babies, candy cane borders, and crystal snowflakes gleaming from my small tree. It's like he saw how beautiful I'd made everything, and the next day, he dumped a ton of money for tacky decor.

And I won't lie, some of it is funny. But that sort of stuff should be indoors. I have tacky Christmas things inside, away from curious eyes. I'm a nicknack whore. I can't stop buying them — especially the seasonal ones. But Theo Kase is wrecking the look of our street!

To my dismay, he crosses the road, walking straight for my truck, too. He reaches the driver's side before me, and, knowing it's unlocked, opens the door.

"Ruby would be just fine," I say, discouraging the new nickname, but I immediately slam my eyes shut, shaking my head. The jerk has me so confused, I finally told him we could be first-name friendly. Flustered, I amend, "Ms. Warner. You may call me Ms. Warner."

He leans against my door, one hand along the top of the frame, and he cocks his head to one side. He rubs his stubbled jaw, and he doesn't hide the way his blue eyes drift inappropriately down my body.

"I don't know," he drawls. "Red hair, red dress, rosy red lips on most occasions. We could wrap you in a pretty, red bow, but I already know you like to wrap yourself in other pretty, red things."

My left eye twitches, and Theo drags his eyes back to my face. His intensity is stifling, and the open street suddenly seems way too close and intimate. I hesitate, flicking my gaze between him and the front seat of my truck.

"That is highly inappropriate, Mr. Kase," I say, but my throat is dry, and my words die on my lips, barely uttered. It's too much. His words are too much, bringing back flashes of heated gazes and warm hands.

God, I sound like a breathy bimbo. That's probably why his eyes are dropping back down to my cleavage, imagining things he's already seen.

I'll admit that was my fault.

I'd had a dry spell. No dates for six months. And anyone who goes a long period without dating can tell you that one might find themselves very comfortable in their aloneness. My comfortable but stagnant life was becoming unhealthy. I needed to mix it up, or at least, feel sexy again.

Theo Kase moved in one weekend in February. My sporadic decision to buy expensive, scarlet lingerie with lace and tiny bows happened in March.

The incident happened in April.

It was late, just after sundown, and the streetlights were glowing. I'd been awaiting a package — a new shipment of plates for work. As soon as the delivery truck left my box on the curb, I wrapped my lingerie-clad body in my pink, fuzzy robe, confident that no one would suspect a thing.

My neighbors were used to me rummaging around my small garden in all sorts of comfortable clothes, and they'd all seen my robe. No one should have noticed my bare legs or freshly moisturized skin.

All I had to do was walk to the curb, pick up my box, and walk back inside.

Except Theo Kase had moved in two months prior, and I'd made him cookies as a kind, neighborly gesture. We hadn't spoken since — we'd both been busy — and he pulled into his driveway right as I reached my rickety mailbox. The large package was on the ground right next to it.

It was obviously too heavy for me. I tried to hide my struggle as I picked it up, but Theo likes to pretend he's a gentleman sometimes. He hollered a greeting, rushed to help me, and I was so grateful. I followed him as he carried it right inside.

As he turned, standing in my small entryway, to ask where I wanted the giant box, it happened.

I turned to shut the front door as I asked him whether he wanted something to drink, but my robe caught on the shoe bench that sits just inside. Suddenly, I was naked. Or, standing in bright red lingerie that swirled sparingly over my breasts and didn't hide anything down below. I'm not exactly sure what part of me he focused on the most, but I do know he could see my nipples. I know this because he uttered one stupid word.

Nice.

Nice? Nice?!

I'd gaped at him, but the word rubbed me in just the wrong way.

"Nice!" I'd burst. "This isn't nice! This is hot — bangable! I'm bangable, dammit!"

It was not my proudest moment.

There was a moment of brief confusion where I realized Theo Kase was completely willing, and I forcefully pushed him out my door, straight onto his ass on my front porch, yelling at him while I bounced agitatedly in my bright, red lingerie.

And the jerk had seemed completely enamored by the whole thing.

Now, our interactions are like some twisted game as if he's trying to get under my skin as payback. Lacy, perky, C-cup, and ribbons were all things he called me over the next few weeks. Then, the nicknames got creative. In all fairness, Red is the most normal thing he's called me.

Except, the lingerie was red, and I know he means it as a barb.

"I'm not sure how calling a redhead, Red, is inappropriate," Theo says, his eyes finding mine again. His jaw tenses, and his eyes glow with amusement. "You're decked out in red, too. Pretty dress."

I narrow my eyes, not breaking his gaze.

He knows exactly what he's doing.

"Mr. Kase, it is Christmas Eve," I say, straightening my spine, so I stand an inch taller. I do my best to glower at him, but he's still at least half a foot taller than me. He grins like I'm some sort of rabid chipmunk, unable to attack from an invisible cage.

That invisible cage was manners and my reputation and living in an adorable house on my favorite street. I don't need my neighbors talking about how I lost it and tried to rip the new guy's face off.

When Theo continues to stare at me, grinning, I go on.

"Today is a very big day. I have a full day of work, and I've volunteered to help during the festival tonight. I would appreciate it if, for once, we could go our separate ways without this exhausting verbal tango."

"The tango is full of passion," Theo says, and his grin turns feral as he lifts one dark brow. "Are you saying you're left exhausted after our passionate encounters?"

If he needed one more reason to call me Red, now he has it. My cheeks flame, but that embarrassment turns to fury. I'm pretty sure I have steam rising from my scalp as my temper flares.

"Goodbye, Mr. Kase," I snap, and I step unnervingly close to him, so I can make it into my driver's seat.

Theo stands there, grinning at his shoes while I tuck my skirt underneath myself. He probably only looks down so the neighbors won't realize what a scoundrel he is, but he closes the door of my truck with surprising care. If I hadn't known him for so long, I would think he was careful on purpose, knowing how important the ancient hand-me-down truck from my uncle is.

I'm so caught off guard by the gentle, firm closing of the door that I almost don't hear him murmur, "Goodbye, Ruby. Have a good day."

I open my mouth, flustered by his departure. Usually, he has one last quip.

I grab the handle to manually roll down the window and start cranking. I'd spent part of the morning thawing out my truck, and it hadn't snowed since yesterday morning, so it's an easy task. I start to call after him, ready for round two, but he trots up his porch steps and disappears through his front door.

I frown.

That's not like him.

That's not like him at all.

Wrinkling my nose, I recognize the twinge of guilt that sparks in my chest. I force myself to shove away my worries, knowing it's better to let this moment go.

Still, it *is* Christmas Eve. All he did was throw a half-melted snowball at my house and wish me a good day.

I might have been a little cold towards him.

I stare at his front door for another minute, but when he doesn't reemerge, I start up my truck and head to work.

TWO

THEO

Ruby Warner is the type of woman that you never forget. I knew it from the moment I saw her standing at my doorstep, a wide smile across her face as she extended a tray of chocolate chip cookies to me. She was beautiful, but I quickly learned that was the least interesting thing about her.

An early riser, I've always started my days with coffee outside, enjoying whatever weather life provides and letting it set the tone for the day. I felt in sync with nature when my mindset matched the world around me, and life has always flowed in a positive direction when I feel connected.

Back home, in the busy city where my mom and sister thrive, running a book bar that caters to people who like pink, fluffy things, reading, and booze, I started my days at four. It was the easiest way to avoid people.

So, I was surprised when I stepped onto my front porch at four in the morning, the day after devouring half a tray of cookies, to see that the sleepy town of Bellington wasn't as sleepy as I'd imagined it to be.

Ruby was painting the railing of her porch, adding swirls of jade vines and subtle, deep purple flowers. This wouldn't have seemed too strange, but it was February and freezing.

The next time I saw her, she was rapidly waving her front door back and forth, cursing because she'd lit a fire and forgotten to open her chimney. Smoke poured so rapidly from her house, I'd thought it was on fire, but our other neighbor — Jamison, who lives right next to me — waved and shook his head as he retreated from her property, warning me not to intervene.

The third time I saw her, she was walking two cats on leashes. Later, I learned they belonged to Mrs. Barry down the street, and Ruby did this twice a month despite being allergic to cats.

The fourth time I saw her, she was in a fuzzy, pink bathrobe, and I couldn't help but smile. My mom and sister would have loved it — they probably would have loved *her* — and I was halfway towards her to say hello before I realized how inappropriate that might seem. She was wrestling a package when she noticed my approach, so I quickly offered to help. I scooped it up and carried it inside.

Then, I saw all of her.

The image of Ruby in skimpy lingerie will forever be engrained on my brain.

I thought she was trying to come onto me. I had my

hands on her hips, trying to process her rambling, before I realized she was mortified, had no interest in me, and hadn't noticed me nearly as frequently as I had noticed her.

Getting thrown on my ass by Ruby Warner and cursed at while the swells of her breasts battled for dominance over the lace material, the muscles of her smooth thighs shifting in the warm light of her home, was one of the best moments of my life despite how mad it made her.

I meant no harm — really, I didn't — and I took my hands off her as soon as I realized the misunderstanding.

But I'm deplorable.

Unworthy.

And Ruby Warner is spectacular.

She's the ruler of her own life and can take down a man who's got at least sixty pounds on her.

She walks cats, for Christ's sake.

Ruby Warner can do anything.

And she absolutely can't stand me.

I should make amends — I want to make amends. But there's something about the way she gets so flustered, and the dwindling control she has over that simmering temper does something to me.

It's fun to irritate her.

But I also care about her.

She's a good person.

Which is why I wait until she drives down the street before I run outside and jump in my Audi. I doubt my car is suitable for the coming weather, but I've been told by several people that the snow almost always melts away.

There are only a few weeks a year where it sticks. The roads are clear for now, and the only hazard on it is Ruby Warner in her rickety, old truck.

I saw her with a roll of duct tape, looking under her hood one day. Ever since, I've tried to follow her to work. It helps that her old-fashioned diner is a short walk from the contemporary restaurant I've opened near the center of town.

When I realized she was the owner of Maddy's, the lingerie incident had already happened. Opening day of my place, Dish & Dally, seemed like the final nail in the coffin, dashing any hope of making amends. Her quaint, charming place had less business that day, but it quickly went back to normal. I just wish she'd see that there was space for both of us, red undergarments aside.

As I drive down Winterberry Road, I'm relieved to see her truck parked in front of Maddy's. I pass it, keeping my gaze ahead because the last time I peered towards the windows for a glimpse of her, she flipped me off. I pull into my marked parking space in front of Dish & Dally, knowing I have plenty of time before our doors open. I go for my usual walk around the town square, and I enjoy watching the different businesses slowly come to life.

Later in the day, while the lunch rush is in full-swing, the silver-and-glass doors of my place open, and Stacy Moore walks into the building. She's all legs with one of the most welcoming smiles I've ever seen, which works extra well for her since she's the mayor's wife. She makes her way straight towards to back, and I intercept her, knowing she has a bad habit of sticking her finger in tasty looking foods.

"Mrs. Moore!" I call, opening my arms in greeting.

She immediately throws her arms out, shuffling her feet as she changes directions. In her high heels, she's nearly as tall as I am, but she hugs everyone, even those she towers over. She gives me a quick embrace and starts patting my shoulder, leading me towards my own kitchen.

"I just came to confirm that you are, in fact, bringing the pies," she says, her voice high and whimsical. She flicks her attention around as if searching for the pies herself, and her blonde hair slaps me in the face.

I rub my eye, wrinkling my nose with a smile.

"Yes, Mrs. Moore," I drawl, but she knows it's in good humor. "As I promised yesterday, you don't have a thing to worry about. They're safely in the walk-in. I've set aside a whole section of the shelves just for your order. I can take you back to look at them, if you'd like."

"Oh, no need to do that," she says, dismissing my offer with a wave. "I just wanted to double check. Harold has been overly busy with the holiday season, so I just want to do my part to make sure the festivities go well tonight. The winter festival is one of his favorite events to attend."

She nods as if reassuring herself that all will go according to plan. She's ordered several dozen pies for tonight, and we don't really do pies, but she'd been so damn welcoming when Dish & Dally opened. She has weekly lunches with her friends, and she's always bringing in new people. Her and her husband do a lot to make sure the town's businesses thrive, and she treated me, a newcomer, no different. Saying no when she asked if we could provide the pies was not an option, so Dish & Dally now does pie.

"I'll be delivering them personally, and Timmy will be assisting with serving tonight," I tell her, nodding to the teenage kid walking by with a busser's bin. He smiles, giving her a nod.

"He's a sweet boy," Stacy says, approving. "I just hope I'm not forgetting anything. I need to check on the hot chocolate next..."

"We can do hot chocolate," I offer, shrugging.

Stacy's face lights up, her eyes gleaming. "Could you? Oh, that would be great! We always have peppermint hot chocolate, but I always liked it the classic way. With marshmallows?"

"Marshmallows aren't a problem," I say, chuckling at her enthusiasm. She nearly knocks me over when she throws her arms around me again, thanking me.

"Well, I better be going," she says, shuffling around like she's in a rush. "Everything starts at seven, so get there early enough to be completely set up. Be sure to say hi to Harold tonight!"

"Will do, Mrs. Moore," I say, nodding and waving after her retreating form.

She blows a kiss, tossing her arm dramatically, her signature departure for everyone.

I keep walking towards the door even though she's long gone by the time I reach it. Still, I use her exit as an excuse to catch some fresh air. I step outside, inhaling deeply and anticipating the snow that's soon to fall.

I peer down the street, and I have a clear view of Maddy's on the opposite side of the road. Ruby's truck is still there, but there's a glare on the windows, so I can't see inside the building.

For a moment, I contemplate heading over there to ask whether she needs help during the festival tonight. I know she said she volunteered, but I don't know what she's doing. But I don't want her to dread going if she finds out I'll be there. I'm hoping tonight — with the Christmas spirit in the air — I'll be able to put a dent in that impenetrable wall she's thrown up between us.

I sigh, stealing one last glance towards her restaurant before I turn and go inside. I have a good feeling about tonight despite her brittle attitude towards me this morning. Something's happening tonight — I can feel it. One way or another, I will get her to soften towards me. One way or another, Ruby Warner might not hate me by the end of the night.

It's Christmas Eve. A miracle could surely happen.

THREE

RUBY

The winter festival is something I look forward to every year. It's not just about embracing the holidays and bringing the community together. For me, it's one of the few connections I still have to Aunt Maddy and Uncle Joe.

The restaurant, the house, the truck, and this festival. It's a life they built for me, but there's moments when their absence stings. The festival always takes away that sting.

Aunt Maddy would make her famous, peppermint hot chocolate every year, and I've carried on the tradition, using her exact recipe. It can feel lonely without them by my side, but the town seems to remember how involved they were with the festival. Many people take the opportunity to share fond memories with me, making small talk in the best way possible over steaming cups of chocolate.

I need it. I so desperately need the festival by this time of year. And this year, three years after their passing, I feel like I need it more than usual. The holidays never feel complete until the festival.

Jenny and Lindsey, my friends even though they technically work for me, help me load everything up. We changed clothes, so we're wearing matching red, velvet dresses with white trim. It's what all the other festival workers will be wearing. The guys wear velvet pants and vests over a sweater, and it's ridiculous, but it's fun.

We reach Winterberry Estate in no time, and we maneuver through the carnival rides and booths that are set up all over the property. We go right into the thick of things, not too far from the large colonial home that's lit up inside and out, lined with twinkling lights and dotted with Christmas trees.

Jenny and Lindsey have helped me set up before, so opening the tables and preparing everything goes fast. We spend the rest of our prep time laughing and talking and catching up.

Before we know it, the festival is in full swing. Kids are laughing, people are mingling, and it's everything you could want from this time of year. The flow of people to our spread of tables is slow but steady, and I get lost in it, embracing the spirit of the night.

Everything is going according to plan until Mrs. Barry walks by, cradling a Styrofoam cup.

"No need to walk the cats tomorrow, dear," she says, greeting me with an open arm.

I hug her, pulling back with a concerned grin. "You sure? I don't mind. I know they fight if they don't get out of the house for a while. Their shoes aren't that hard to put on."

I should feel bad for lying on Christmas Eve, but she doesn't need to be plagued with stories of scratches and near death-by-cat moments.

"I have a new, special friend that's going to build a gym for them," she says, winking conspiratorially. "He's going to put up ramps and platforms along the walls, so they can exercise all day long."

I chuckle, not sure I want any more details than that about her new, special friend. Her wink implies things I don't want to consider. I've known her so long; this woman feels like a grandmother to me. I want her to be happy, but there are some things you can't forget hearing.

"Very good hot chocolate this year," she coos, patting me on the arm. "I always liked that peppermint stuff, but it's nice you're serving a classic this year. Really puts me in the spirit."

She walks away before I have time to fully process her words.

I spin on my heels, staring after her.

"Classic?" I cast a look towards Jenny and Lindsey. Both look away, but not before Jenny's eyes meet mine. The guilt and worry are so evident there, so I walk towards her. "What did Mrs. Barry mean by a classic option?"

Jenny smiles, her teeth on full display, while panic flashes in her eyes.

"It's not a big deal," she says, and she dips her eyes to our cups that all reek of peppermint. "People are still coming to our booth. And everyone's happy!"

Lindsey doesn't look my way, but I glance at her at just the right moment. Her eyes flash across the grass, down the hill towards a large crowd.

"Are you saying someone else is giving out hot chocolate?"

Their silence is telling.

Scoffing, I smooth out my dress and start down the hill towards the mass of people. I glance back at my friends, trying to convey that it's no big deal. I'm just going to have a friendly chat. Perhaps, whoever it is will want to move their booth closer, so the usual crowd will still make its way to our tables. They're closer to the entrance, so it makes sense why I haven't seen as many people as usual by this point in the night.

The air is shifting, snow coming soon, and it feels like the night itself is holding its breath as I reach the crowd. I push my way through, excusing myself and frowning at the slices of pie that look frustratingly delicious. The last part of the crowd finally breaks away, and I come face to face with an elaborate stand of pies and cups of coco.

Through a small window, a teenage boy smiles at me, lifting his brows. "Pumpkin, apple, or chocolate?"

He's wearing the same thing as all the other festival workers, but he looks strangely familiar. For some reason, I can't place him. Perhaps I would recognize him if he were in his usual attire...

"What?" I ask, shaking my head in confusion.

"We have other pies, but it's going to take a few minutes to get them ready," he says, nodding over his shoulder.

Behind him, someone else in matching festival attire is bent over, rearranging boxes beneath a table.

"Offer the hot chocolate, Timmy," a gruff voice says.

A gruff, *familiar* voice.

Suddenly, everything becomes crystal clear.

"You!" I shout, making everyone around me jump. Even the teenager in front of me looks startled, and he sidesteps like he doesn't want to be standing between us. "You did this on purpose!"

Stooped beneath the table, the man bounces a little and bumps his head. Delight shimmers through me, and I lick my lips like his injury is more delicious than any pie he could have given me.

Theo Kase mutters curses under his breath, rubbing the back of his head as he turns around, dislodging the Santa hat he's wearing. He frowns, but as soon as he sees me, his entire face lights up.

"Oh," he says, smiling like he's happy to see me. "Hey, Red."

The casual greeting dumps ice water all over the small thrill of delight I'd experienced. I scowl, folding my arms.

"You stole hot chocolate," I snap, glaring at him.

He cocks his head, that smile stretching with amusement.

"Careful now," he warns. "If you don't make any sense, I might have to check you out. Don't want there to be something loose up there."

He taps the side of his head and winks at me.

"You stole hot chocolate," I say again, folding my arms

over my chest. "We already provide hot chocolate for the festival. You're not supposed to be serving it with your... pie."

As I say the word, the teenager from before passes out more slices from the side tables, ignoring the booth window I've taken over. I can't lie. It all looks delicious. I shake my head, trying to maintain focus.

Theo stares at me, and when he meets my gaze, his smile falters.

"Mrs. Moore wanted more options," he says, uncertain. His brows tug together, his lips turning down.

I level my gaze, holding his stare.

"You did this on purpose," I challenge. I don't give him time to respond before I turn on my heels and march up the hill.

If he wants to spoil Christmas, fine. But he's not going to spoil *my* Christmas. I can pretend he doesn't exist. I've been doing exactly that for months, aside from the moments that he intrusively inserts himself into my life.

"Ruby!" he calls, and my name on his lips makes my spine go rigid.

I dash up the hill, running away from him. I throw myself into the night, mixing and mingling, and taking what I'm given and trying not to feel like something's been stolen from me.

It doesn't work.

Theo Kase is a selfish, invasive pig.

I watched him, down the hill, despite my best efforts to

ignore his existence. He gave out more salacious grins than slices of pie. He's exactly what I expected him to be. Horrible.

The night dwindles fast with less people venturing our way. It was a good night, and I should appreciate the people that came by, but I can't help but feel like everything sweet has turned sour. The lights seem too bright, and the crisp air feels biting. It finally starts to snow, and it feels like the universe is mocking me. This night isn't what I wanted or needed it to be.

I pack up early without any complaints from Jenny or Lindsey. They both give me sympathetic grins as they fill my truck with tepid chocolate, staring after me as I wave and drive off.

On the way home, snow coming down all around, something takes over me.

I can't stand it anymore.

Theo Kase has got to go, but I know he won't. He lives here, and he's settled now. He's set up a life, and apparently, he's determined to thrive no matter how it affects me. He's a real-life villain, stealing the spirit of every season all year long.

So, with my dwindling Christmas spirit, I think I lose my mind.

I pull onto our street as the snow continues falling, idling up to the curb in front of his house, not even glancing at mine. I look at his lawn decorations, his yard fresh with snow, and I wrinkle my nose as I realize the final touch it needs.

FOUR
THEO

I look around as the night is ending. Lights are being shut off, carnival rides are starting to send people away so workers can pack up, and families are going home. It was a perfect night and exactly what I needed. Everything went just right.

Everything except Ruby.

She was so damn mad, her attitude all huffy. I had no idea what she was talking about at first. She always looks so angry when she talks to me, so I just assumed it was another cute spat.

But there was something in her expression, something like genuine hurt and confusion, that punched me in the gut and left something heavy and dreadful over my heart.

She looked at me like I betrayed her.

She thinks I hurt her on purpose.

The hot chocolate was... whatever. It didn't mean anything to me. To any sane, normal person, it wouldn't be a big deal. But this is a woman that puts shoes on cats

24

and paints outdoors in freezing temperatures. Nothing she does lacks passion.

And I took something she was passionate about.

I drive home, reciting different apologies along the way, but none of them feel good enough. If I'd known she was in charge of the hot chocolate — if I'd known it was something important to her — I never would have brought any. It would just be so much easier to convince her that's true if I knew why she was so distraught over a hot drink.

"I should have offered to bring eggnog," I grumble, turning onto our street.

Snowfall started shortly after Ruby stormed away. Much to my car's dismay, it seems to be sticking around. It's beautiful. The perfect atmosphere for a genuine apology and cracking that hard, outer shield Ruby wields. My headlights cut through the night, and I'm surprised when I see the dark shape of Ruby's truck parked in front of my house, on the opposite side of the street than her usual parking spot.

I slow, preparing to turn into my driveway. Before I'm able to, a blur of red sprints in front of my car.

Ruby, with arms raised to shield her eyes from my headlights, flicks me off, sticks out her tongue, and darts towards her own yard.

"What the hell?" I bark. I'd stomped on my brakes hard, and my heart is still pounding. I'm not used to driving in snow. I could have hit her. I roll down the window and call, "What was that?!"

"Exactly what you deserve!" she shouts, making impressive time in her boots.

I put my car in park, shutting it off without even bothering to pull into my driveway. I'm close enough to the curb that it shouldn't matter, but I almost fall on my ass when my shoe hits the pavement.

"Where are you going?" I yell, watching as she skips up the steps to her porch like it's some sort of sanctuary. "What'd you do, Red?"

"Stop calling me that!" She crosses her arms, pouting at me from her halo of porch light. She shifts on her feet, and the light illuminates her just enough that I can tell when her attention drifts towards my front door, her hair gleaming with the movement.

What the hell did she do?

I stalk between my car and her truck, dread coiling in my stomach. It doesn't take long to figure out why she was running.

"It's a penis!" I yell. I shoot a look over my shoulder, then glance back at the hundreds of cups on my walkway, a dark mass of chocolate amongst the white snow. She's arranged them into what is, undeniably, a dick and balls, no lids in sight. They're close enough together that if I knock over one, the rest could fall like dominos. "Children live on this street!"

"You have a pole dancing reindeer as a decoration! A giant dick shouldn't bother you!"

"It does bother me!" I wrinkle my nose, huffing out a breath and contemplating how long it's going to take me to pick them up. I should just get a shovel and scoop it all into the trash. "This is bad, Ruby!"

I turn to find her stomping down her steps, so I aim to meet her. I stride straight for her, cutting into her yard and feeling more aggressive than I should. But she's gotten under my skin. She's honestly pissed me off.

"This is childish," I condone, pointing at the mess she's left me.

She glares up at me, not backing down an inch.

"If you don't like it, you can leave," she snorts, eyes flashing with challenge.

"Leave?" I ask, and I shake my head, unable to keep myself from smirking at the way she's pushing back at me. "Oh, Red, if you thought this would get me to pack up and leave town, you've got another thing coming. I've been nice until now, and I'm still trying to make a good impression on the town. This little stunt has only made me even more committed to my vision."

Committed to my vision? All I want to do is live on a quiet street, enjoy slow mornings, and run my restaurant. But the way Ruby is looking at me, her green eyes gleaming, makes me want to pull that boiling frustration right out of her.

"A good impression?" she scoffs, shaking her head. She plants her hands on her hips and inches towards me. "The only impression you leave is slimy and... misshapen. It's not a very good one."

"Misshapen?" I ask, unable to keep my lips from turning up. "Do I not even seem like a man to you? I'm just some blight on your..."

I trail off, my eyes drifting up, over her head.

"What the hell?"

"What?" Ruby snaps, whirling towards her house. Her eyes land on the exact thing I'm staring at, but her mind shifts a thousand miles in the opposite direction. "Ugh! Is this your doing?"

There's a man on top of her house, wearing full Santa gear and tugging a strand of Christmas lights over the railing of what looks like a very realistic sleigh.

"You just couldn't help yourself, could you?" Ruby drawls, stalking towards her house. The loose strand of lights hangs down over the edge of her roof, just low enough for her to reach the end of it. "You can't stand beautiful things, and you had to put something tacky on my roof."

"Ruby, wait," I say, finally snapping out of my surprised stupor. The man acts like he hasn't noticed us yet, but that doesn't mean he isn't dangerous. She's getting way too close to him, and that sleigh could slide right off her roof.

"Ha, ha," she snaps, and she grips the light strand in both hands. "Lucky for me, you never quite finish a job, do you?"

Before I can stop her, she pulls, and she pulls hard.

"Ruby!" I shout, running towards her.

The sleigh — because it's definitely a full-sized, heavy sleigh — doesn't budge, but the man shouts in surprise. Ruby looks up, eyes growing as her mouth forms a perfect O, and we both watch in horror as whoever is up on her roof flails his arms. He turns, glances down at us as his white beard blows in the wind, and topples backwards.

Ruby screams, covering her mouth and bouncing up and down, nearly drowning out my curses. Then, she takes off for her backyard before I can grab her.

I run after her, calling her name, but as she yanks open her gate, an icy chill wraps around me. It dries out my words, rendering me speechless. And there, in the middle of her snow-covered yard, the Santa imposter is sprawled out, not moving.

"Oh, no, no, no," Ruby says, her voice going all high and squeaky. She turns to look at me, panic flushing her cheeks. "Is he dead? Oh, my gosh, is he dead?"

"No, he isn't dead," I groan, stepping past her, so she's not the closest one to whoever this crazy guy is that was on her roof. I get a good look at him, surprised by how much he looks like the cartoonish Santas from my childhood. He even has the rosy cheeks. "He didn't fall that far. He's probably faking it."

Ruby scoffs as if she's offended by my lack of concern. Then, just as I'm turning to face her, she shrieks, covering her mouth as her green eyes go even wider.

"And that?" she asks, bouncing and pointing towards the red velvet-clad stranger. "Is he faking that?"

"Faking what?" I snap, whirling to see what's got her so freaked out. It feels like she ruptured my right ear drum.

I don't immediately see what's got her so spooked. She's still waving her hand towards the unmoving man, and she's bouncing so much, she nearly whacks me in the face with her arm. She moves closer, and I feel her body press against my triceps as she huddles against me like I'm some sort of shield.

It's distracting. So distracting that I glance over my shoulder at her twice before I finally zero in on the unmoving man.

"What the…"

I know that the fall from the roof most likely wouldn't kill someone. They'd have to have pretty bad luck. And I know it's cold, the snow freshly fallen, but that doesn't explain what I'm seeing.

Dusting his red ensemble, skin, white hair, and beard, a thin layer of frost and ice takes shape.

"What is that?" I ask, creeping closer as the thin layer starts to gleam and… glow. It's glowing — or, the guy is. Yellow light seems to rise around him, encasing him until I can hardly make out his face.

"Did you do this?" Ruby asks, stepping up to my side. "Whatever you did, this isn't funny!"

I'm about to tell her that whatever this is, isn't something I could make happen. Wind sweeps in behind us, blasting through the open gate so fiercely that Ruby grabs onto me to keep from falling. I clutch her forearms, trying to steady her, and our eyes lock together in a moment of panic as a strange, electrical hum fills the air.

Blinding light comes from the man's direction, and we turn and squint against it. I raise one arm to shield my eyes, but just as I look at him, something bursts. There's a flash, energy crackles like lightning through the night, and something shatters. A sound like fragile glass raining down fills the night like a symphony of high-pitched jingles.

Shocked, I look at Ruby, and we slowly turn to look at what remains.

There, in the snow, is an empty Santa suit covered with shattered ice. And floating down to land in the center, glowing golden and bright, is what looks like a handwritten letter.

"This is a bad dream," Ruby mutters, dropping her hold on me. Her face goes blank, and her shoulders go limp as she stares at the mess in a daze. "A really weird, bad dream."

Before I'm completely pulled into that belief, I move forward, swatting stray Santa ice crystals from the air. I bend down, reaching straight for the golden paper.

As soon as I touch it, it fades, taking on the look of old parchment. As I lift it, I realize it's two sheets. One is completely blank, but the other looks like a childish sketch of the town. Snow crunches beneath a boot, and I look over to see Ruby moving towards me. She snatches the blank paper out of my hand.

"Lacking in Christmas cheer," she says, staring at the page, "you two have been at it all year."

She rolls her eyes, staring at me. I frown down at her, then glance at the blank paper. She snorts and lifts it in front of herself again.

"You've wrecked Christmas — that much can't be undone. Unless you work together — hurry, you better run."

"Are you reading that?" I ask, trying to take the paper from her. She jerks away from me, holding it out of reach.

"Four glowing stars will revive my holiday cheer. Find them all to save my life — and Christmas — this year." Ruby frowns, turning the blank paper over as if looking for more words. "Is this some kind of joke?"

"Give me that," I say, grabbing the paper out of her hand before she can stop me. I turn it back and forth, squinting at the page. "There's nothing on here."

"You just have to hold it at an angle," she says, grabbing the corner of the page.

As soon as her fingers touch the paper, golden letters swirl across it. Angled towards the light of her house, the ink gleams just enough to make out the short passage she'd read. But I could have sworn nothing was there before she touched it.

I gingerly tug the paper from her hand, watching in awe as the letters slowly vanish.

"Are you not seeing this?" I ask, giving her a quizzical look.

She frowns at me, clearly not seeing the change at all.

"You need to stop messing with me," she says, her brows drawn together. Then, she reaches for the map in my hands, taking it before I can stop her.

I watch as everything on the surface swirls around, landing in different spots.

"The map just changed," I mutter, struggling to comprehend that this is real and not a dream as she claims. Things are starting to feel stranger and stranger by the second.

"I told you to stop messing with me," she growls, holding the map in front of herself. She twists the paper this way and that, trying to make sense of what she's seeing. "Whatever you did to plan this, it's ridiculous. I'm going inside."

"Ruby!" I call after her as she starts to walk to her back door. She ducks her head, eyes locked on the nonsensical map, and lets herself into her house.

FIVE

RUBY

I burst through my back door, clutching the magical map between my hands. Staring at it, I wield it little more than an inch from my face like it might blur out my periphery, so the craziness of this night doesn't sink in.

This is a dream. A Theo-headache induced, strange dream. I drank too much of my own hot chocolate, and the sugar made me high. It's the only explanation.

Behind me, Theo catches the door, stopping it from hitting him in the face, unfortunately. The last thing I want is to welcome him into my home, but this is a dream, and my subconscious is reminding me that no matter what I do, I'll never be rid of him. He's infiltrated every part of my life, and now he's ruining Christmas.

That's why Santa exploded in my backyard. In my dream. Very realistically.

"Ruby, let me see," Theo repeats for the umpteenth time.

The jerk actually has the nerve to march into my house

and reach for the paper I'm holding as if he has some sort of right to it. Dream Theo is very much like Real Theo.

"You don't need to see," I say calmly, turning the map this way and that. Nothing makes sense to me. It's like the whole town is switched around and jumbled up. Dreams are like that though. Details are skewed. It makes sense that this is a dream.

"The letter said we needed to work together," Theo says, and he's annoyingly calm. He stops a few feet away, looking extra large next to the reindeer and elf figurines I have propped against each other in the small hall. "Let me see the map. I can help."

"If you are a figment of my brain, you will only make things worse," I mutter, shaking my head. I squint at the map, noting how an entire park is in the wrong location. I steal one look at Theo, considering letting him help, but there's red fabric protruding from the crook of his arm, and it takes me a second to realize it's the Santa costume. It's clearly a reminder from my subconscious that everything going wrong is his fault. He's been caught red-handed! Or, red-armpitted. "If you insist on being ever-present in my mind, it would mean a lot if you could dispose of the dead Santa evidence."

I half expect the vibrant fabric to evaporate from sight. It doesn't though. He just glances at it with a frown before shifting to hold it in his free hand.

"This doesn't feel real," he murmurs. "We should probably hide this. This feels like some sort of crime."

A wild, mangled cry slips up my throat.

"A crime?" I burst, almost laughing at his shocked expression. "It's Christmas, and we just murdered Santa Claus. I would say a crime is a bit of an understatement."

"It's Christmas Eve," he amends. "Don't be dramatic. He's not dead. This is just some weird holiday snow magic. I'm pretty sure that map is a key to fixing things."

"Holiday snow magic?" I sneer. I let out an incredulous laugh. "This is a dream, and you won't even leave me alone in my sleep! You've been a curse since you moved in. Everything was going fine until you got here!"

A deep line forms between Theo's brows as they pinch together, and the twist of his mouth doesn't seem quite right. The emotion looks too earnest on him, too real. Genuine regret shines in his eyes as he studies me, and heat licks at my cheeks so suddenly that I have to look away to keep my eyes from stinging.

"If this is a dream," he starts, taking a step forward. "Then, dream me better, Red. Let me be helpful. Let me look at the map." He drops the loose Santa fabric onto a small table of knickknacks as he approaches.

Exhaustion weighs on my shoulders, partly because it took a lot of energy to arrange all those hot chocolate cups into a giant penis, but mostly because I just really needed tonight to go perfectly, and it didn't.

"Everything is in the wrong spot," I mutter, extending the map towards him. I drag my eyes up, meeting his for just a moment before I focus on the paper between us.

The moment Theo touches it, something zings through me like an alarm. My spine goes rigid like someone ran an icicle down the center of my back, and my skin buzzes with electricity. My eyes flick to his, and I see a note of surprise on his face as if he feels it too. When I look back at the map, everything has changed.

The town is drawn as it should be, everything in its place. And there, hovering over Firefly Hill, one of the largest parks in town, is a glowing, golden star.

"Firefly Hill," I murmur, staring in amazement.

"What was that?"

"Firefly Hill," I reiterate. I point with my finger, glancing up at him. I know he's new in town, but he can read. It should be obvious.

"What about it?" he asks, frowning.

"The star," I say, tapping my finger against it. I peer up at him, watching as his frown only deepens. Slowly, understanding dawns. "You can't see it..."

Theo moves his hand, letting go of the map.

"No, no, no!" I say as the black ink starts to swirl into disorder again. The star disappears, and the map becomes a jumbled version of Bellington. "Huh. I guess you have to be touching it."

"That's what she said," he prattles off, and I huff out a laugh. His eyes flick to mine with something like delight since I didn't condemn his stupid joke. He reaches for the paper again, touching it gingerly. "You said there's a star?"

Just as before, ink swirls and moves like magic. The town realigns, and glowing with light, the star hovers over Firefly Hill like a beacon of hope.

"It's right here," I say, touching the spot. "It's the only

star on the map, but I think I'm supposed to go there."

"You mean *we* are supposed to go there," he says, shooting me a look. "The note said we had to work together, and clearly we both have to be touching the map."

Scoffing, I pull the map away from him, rolling my eyes. "I doubt I'll need you. I already know where to go. I'll figure out the rest once I get there."

"The letter said four stars," Theo reminds me, and his words give me pause. "Even if you figure out where that star leads, there's going to be three more."

He's right. I hate that he's right.

"Fine, but we're taking my truck."

"Fine with me," he says, catching me by surprise. He strides past me, leaving the discarded Santa suit in a heap on my precious table.

I huff, grabbing it to throw in a closet. No body, no crime — but a suit left behind... It's better to be safe than sorry.

"I'm going to go throw this upstairs," I say quickly, waving the fabric.

As I do, the fabric unfolds from my hand, another piece of paper tumbling out. I shake the material, frowning because I swear there was... more of it. Tilting my head sideways, I look at the suit again, only to find that it's not a suit, but a miniature Santa bag.

"You've got to be joking," I say. My eyes flick to Theo over the red material, but he stoops to pick up the loose leaf of paper.

"For the stars," he recites, needing no magic this time to see the words that are clearly scrawled across the paper. "You think we have to collect actual stars? Like little ornaments?"

"Who knows," I say, shrugging. I wrap my fingers around the neck of the red, velvet bag and pull the strings. Then, I slip the strings through the belt around my Santa dress that I haven't changed out of. I fasten it tightly to my hip, so it doesn't get lost, feeling strangely like a Mrs. Claus.

"That suits you, Red," Theo says, a smile tugging at the corner of his lip. "You look like Santa's pissed off wife."

I scowl, frustrated that we had the same thought. "Let's just get this over with."

And with that, I stomp towards my front door, patting my keys still in my pocket. Theo follows closely, glancing around my living room as we pass through. He doesn't say anything as I lock the door behind us and stomp down the steps.

When we reach my truck, he lets out a heavy sigh.

"Give me just a minute," he says, and he takes off across his yard.

I watch as he runs to grab a large shovel that's leaning against the side of his house. He runs back to the coffee cups I'd left near his front door, scrapes them into disarray so chocolate spills everywhere, and shoves them all towards his bushes with enough brown snow heaped around them to keep them from blowing away.

"You're helping me pick those up later," he says, jogging back to me.

"It looks like you can handle it yourself," I retort, frustrated that he'd cleaned up the mess so easily, even if only temporarily.

I climb into my truck, watching him expectantly. He looks a little uncertain, eyes flicking between me and the passenger side. Finally, he sighs and opens his own door, slipping into the empty seat.

"You sure you're good to drive in the snow?" he asks, lifting a brow.

I start up my vehicle and take off before giving it time to warm up, careful to pass his car a little too closely, so he flinches and swears.

I laugh, unable to help it.

"This is going to be a long night," he mutters, shaking his head.

"Christmas Eve is always the longest night of the year," I say, training my eyes on the road ahead. "Anticipation makes the seconds tick slower."

"Well, tonight's going to be long for a different reason."

"I hope so," I say. "If we don't find the stars in time, Christmas is doomed."

Uneasy silence settles between us, and Theo shifts in his seat. When he reaches to adjust his air vent, turning the heat towards himself, I click on the radio, letting *Run, Rudolph, Run* fill the car. With the tune urging me forward, I press a little harder on the gas and take us to Firefly Hill.

SIX

THEO

In most charming, little towns, children go to bed early on Christmas Eve. That's what they show in the movies. It's what tired parents wish for. It's what estranged relatives look forward to, so they can grab a drink and break the tension.

In Bellington, no one goes to bed early, apparently. The town has fully embraced the Christmas spirit. Couples are taking strolls and sipping warm drinks, store owners sit out front of their darkened storefronts talking with each other, and children are everywhere, running amok.

But nothing could have prepared me for Firefly Hill.

It's a large park on the west side of town. The playscapes are gigantic, there's beautiful walking trails I explored all spring and summer, and there's several fields that are used throughout the year for all sorts of town and sport events.

But Firefly Hill is a monstrous, never-ending climb from the extra parking lot to the park way above. It's a long stretch of smooth land that expands at a rapid incline. If you were to roll down it, you wouldn't be able to stop.

So, I'm surprised to see hundreds of families gathered to send their children down the hill of doom at lightning speeds that can't possibly be safe.

"That doesn't seem like the best idea," I say as Ruby pulls into the upper parking lot. I'm surprised she finds an available parking space, but I'm not going to acknowledge our luck because I'd just told her I doubted there would be parking left up here. She doesn't rub it in my face either, which is surprising, but I'm not going to question it.

"Did you grow up with pillows strapped to your body?" she asks, laughing. "They're sledding. Where else would you have them sled? It's the best hill in town."

"A five-year-old just went down on a plastic trash can lid," I say, stunned as I stare at the blank space the child used to be. A man smiles and holds his phone steady to take a video as the child most likely plummets to their doom.

"Relax," Ruby groans, waving a dismissive hand. She shuts off her truck and climbs out, and I hurry to follow her. "My aunt and uncle used to bring me every winter. It's only scary the first few times, and the ground levels out pretty good at the bottom. You just can't go too close to the center, or it'll send you straight into the parking lot."

"Your aunt and uncle, huh," I say, storing away that tidbit of information. I don't really know much about Ruby's personal life, and despite tonight's dire situation, I still hope to chip away at her frosty exterior, eventually.

"They probably would have gotten along with my mom. She would have bedazzled your sled and put a fluffy, pink trim on it for you."

Ruby gives me a curious look, a small line between her brows as she appraises me, still moving towards the hill.

"I'm surprised you have a mother," she says, her voice unemotional and detached. "I didn't think crude, vile things came from a womb."

"Oh," I groan, drawing out the sound. "That much hate on Christmas Eve? No wonder Santa lumped us together."

"Shh," Ruby warns, and she comes close enough that she can slap my arm. "Don't say anything else about what we did tonight. It's bad enough you wrecked Christmas. Kids don't need to overhear your crimes."

"Is it our crime or mine?" I ask, unable to keep the bite out of my words. "You seem pretty convinced this is my fault, but you're the one that yanked the guy off the roof."

"Will you be quiet?" Ruby whisper-yells, whirling in front of me. She plants her hands on her hips and stands her ground, glaring. "If you hadn't had such tacky Christmas decorations, or hadn't seemed so determined to wreck everything good in my life, I wouldn't have thought Santa on the roof was your doing. It was a complete accident on my part — a misunderstanding — but none of that would have happened if it weren't for you!"

"And a giant, hot chocolate penis? That's just all part of the Christmas spirit?" I cast a look around, but no one is close enough to overhear us. They're all distracted by the fun on the hill. "I'm not trying to wreck your life, Ruby. I don't even see how anything I've done has affected you."

She lets out a strangled cry, a sound of pure shock and disbelief. Green eyes flick rapidly between mine, and her mouth pops open as she fails to find the words to say. She shakes her head back and forth, the movement small, and her eyes shine.

"You think your new venture in life has no effect on me," she mutters, still shaking her head. "You come into town, start up your trendy business, and probably have no intention of staying long-term. You're from the city. You couldn't make it work there, so you're going to set up shop, get the cash flowing, then crawl back to your old life while your business drains my customers."

"Drains your customers?" I ask, equally stunned. "I specifically altered my menu and spent thousands redesigning the storefront, so it would attract different types of people. Not everyone wants the classic mom-and-pop breakfast every day or a burger at lunch, so I'm giving them something different. Your business slowed down for a week before it went back to normal. Dish & Dally isn't a threat to you."

Ruby opens her mouth, closes it, then sighs through her nose. Her frown deepens. Her head cocks to one side, and her pretty little tongue flicks over her lips, and despite how frustrated I am, that one simple movement reminds me of exactly why we're standing here, whisper-screaming at each other.

I like it when she gets huffy and mad. I am an asshole, and I have been pressing her buttons for months. Of course, she thinks I'm trying to take her happiness away. I've never given her a reason to think otherwise. Until this very moment, she had no idea that I'd adjusted my business plans to make sure they didn't negatively impact her business.

And like the asshole I am, I can't help but stare at those ruby-red lips and imagine burying my face into her neck as they whisper my name into my ear.

"Ruby," I say, and god damn, my voice drops to a place I do not want it. Something pulses down my body, and everything tightens below my waist. I feel my dick rise to attention, and the sight of the subtle change in her face — the confusion shifting to alarm and understanding at the sound of my voice — makes my entire body coil with tension.

"Let's look for the star," I say, unable to keep the gruffness out of my voice. I will my feet to move, to step past her and straight towards the hill, but there's one little part of her argument that doesn't sit right with me. "And I'm not leaving Bellington. I moved here for a reason. Despite what you think of me, I have every intention of staying. Forever."

Wrong. It's completely wrong. The very wrong thing to say.

Ruby, whose exterior was just beginning to crack and crumble, stiffens. That solid wall goes right back up, cracks repairing immediately. That confusion and curiosity that was brewing in her electric eyes hardens, and like cold steel, her gaze cuts right through me.

"Mr. Kase," she says, moving backwards from the progress we'd made with each other. Goodbye, first name familiarity. "Tonight, we're working together. After Christmas, I'm going to do everything I can to make sure you have a very good reason to leave."

She spins in her boots, scanning the crowd in the distance before marching towards it. She doesn't even look to see if I'm following. I trot after her, trying not to overthink the way she's heading straight for the center of the hill, the same spot she said most people avoid because it's too steep. It's exactly what she's aiming for though, and for a good reason.

As we reach the crest of the hill, children and families continue their quests down into the pits of Firefly Hill. I have to admit, she's right. As long as they don't get too close to the center — where we're standing — the makeshift sleds slow down gradually at the bottom. Children laugh, and it makes it easy to imagine how happy her childhood must have been.

Directly in front of us, the fluffy strip of untouched snow looks ready to ride down, not sodden or too hard. Actually, it's kind of tempting...

"There!" Ruby bursts, her voice loud and sudden. She grabs my arm and points down the hill towards the parking lot. Then, because I'm apparently looking in the wrong direction, she rises on her toes, grabs the side of my head, and forcefully moves me to look in another direction. "No, jerk. There — on the light post."

Charming and quaint, the parking lot is lined with old-fashioned looking lights, the individual posts looking borderline gothic and from the Victorian era. They're the same lights that line the street we live on, though I've noticed a few of them have gone out. None of these are dark, but it only takes me a second to realize which one she's talking about.

"You don't think..." I start, but she pulls the map from where she'd folded it into her pocket. She opens it with a flourish and grabs my hand.

As soon as she places my grip where she wants it, electricity courses through me, and I get a sense that she feels something flowing through her too. Her spine straightens, and she steps into me, though I doubt she realizes it. With her back to me, she's practically wrapped in my arm while we hold the map together.

"See!" she says, growing excited. She bounces a little, and I watch her curls bounce up and down over her back. "Look, there's a little light post on the map now. That has to be it!"

"So, you think the star is an actual glowing light?" I ask, frowning and fixing my eyes on the map. "Isn't that kind of weird?"

"This whole night is weird," she says, dismissing my concerns. "Now, we just have to run down there, and — oh no!"

Oh no is right. Wind tears at the families strolling through the lower parking lot, stronger and fiercer than before. I watch as a kid's sled careens towards the left, and he dives into the snow as the wooden vehicle continues down the hill without him. It veers further, almost to the center of the hill, and once it reaches the bottom, it launches itself off a small bump towards the parking lot. It hits the light pole, making it wiggle and...

The light — our questionable starlight — detaches from the pole and floats mysteriously in a void of darkness above the cars.

"Is no one else seeing this?" Ruby asks, sounding panicked. She starts bouncing up and down more rapidly on her toes, and she shifts backwards, bumping into me as she moves up and down and up.

"I've got this," I say, taking a desperate step away from her because she's very warm and very soft, and I could smell mint and what must have been apple-scented shampoo.

Ruby looks over her shoulder at me as she bites her bottom lip, and it's just too damn much. I glance around, find an abandoned plank of wood that will work perfectly fine, and completely lose my mind. I toss it into the snow, watch it slide towards the edge of the hill, and I take off on foot behind it. The wood is just going over the crest when I dive onto it — belly flop, really — and with a grunt, I'm flying.

It is every bit as terrifying and lethal as I expected it to be. Children on sleds are a blur as I move past them — headfirst because I'm an idiot and there was almost no blood left in my brain to make it function properly. I grunt, adjusting the rock-hard pain in my pants that's getting crushed against the harsh wood, but after I fix that, there's nothing left to distract me from the fact that I'm plummeting face first down a hill towards a row of very unyielding cars.

"Ahhh!" I scream, and I don't care that my voice rises in pitch enough that people are probably doing double takes. I'm going to die. I'm going to die, and I've wrecked Christmas, and Ruby Warner is going to hate me forever.

"To the right!" Ruby screams from somewhere behind me. "To the right, Theo! To the right!"

I can't look behind me. All I can do is look ahead and to the right, and Ruby is a genius. That tiny, little lump in the snow — the one the kid's sled flew off of — is in just the right place. It will launch me, but it'll launch me between the cars instead of into them.

"Noooo," I cry out because this is about to hurt like hell, and you can't steer a flat piece of wood. Gripping the edges is impossible, and someone is going to be very upset when it smashes into their car. Fearing death, I throw myself to the right and land on my back. I feel ice and snow slide beneath me, tearing at my back through the Santa vest and white sweater I never changed out of, but I have enough sense to keep my chin tucked towards my chest as I cover my head.

And then I'm airborne. I only feel the lump in the snow for a moment before I'm flailing through the air, arms swinging like a freaking moron. I open my eyes, knowing I'm about to experience a world of pain, and as I look up to the starlit sky, a miracle happens.

That little ball of light hovers above me, and my already

swinging arm moves towards it.

I clutch my hand tight as I pass it, expecting hot, searing pain, but it's like grabbing butter. Something yielding and cool squishes in my hand, and I blink at the yellow glow seeping between my clenched fingers. It distracts me so much that I don't brace myself for the landing.

"Ugh," I grunt as my body slams into the ground. Except, it's not the wet, icy concrete I'd expected. My head snaps back as I bounce and land, and my skull sinks into something white and fluffy and warm. "Uhhnnn."

The sound of pain summons an elderly woman, and she leans over me with panic and concern.

"Are you alright, dear?" she asks in a creaky voice. She looks exactly what I would expect a Mrs. Claus to look like. Not a hot, Ruby version of the character. The classic one — the one holding milk and cookies. Her white hair is swept into a bun with loose spirals hanging free, and she's holding some sort of pie in her hands. "You landed in my wagon."

"I think..." I start, voice strained, "You're holding one of my pies."

The woman blinks her crystal blue eyes and glances at what she's holding. A smile spreads across her face, and she looks back at me. "Are you that fellow that opened that cute, new restaurant in town? Mrs. Moore has been telling me I need to check it out. She gave me this pie of yours! I was meeting my kids here, and we're all going to have a slice. But you're in my wagon."

A little frown slides into place as she takes in my

predicament. Body aching, I force myself to grip the edges of the wagon, and I lift myself up. When I do, I realize it's filled with dozens of blankets. The top one is some sort of white, faux fur, and with it draped across the wagon, the whole thing is almost invisible against the snow.

"Sorry about that," I grunt, and I struggle onto my feet. I don't feel quite sturdy. My legs tremble with adrenaline. "I think your wagon saved my life."

"Oh!" she exclaims, looking quite delighted.

"Oh my gosh!" another voice squeals, and this time it comes from close behind.

Ruby has made her way to the bottom of the hill, and she runs up behind me, throwing her arms around my waist.

"I thought you were dead," she huffs, and I'm surprised to feel the relief in her body as she sags against my back. "For real, you were headed straight for the grill of that truck. I said I wanted you to leave! Not that I wanted you to throw yourself towards certain death!"

Almost imperceptibly, her arms tighten around my waist.

"Christmas time is the best time to make amends," the lady says, observing us closely.

Ruby drops her hold around me as soon as she realizes we have an audience, and she clears her throat, sweeping stray, copper tangles of hair from her face as she comes to stand by my side.

"You and your husband make a lovely couple," the woman says, smiling at Ruby as she makes a large assumption. "Clearly, you're destined to be. I saw the way you ran down that hill! Now, *that* is what love looks like."

She smiles, proud of herself for coming to such conclusions as her eyes bounce back and forth between us.

"Thank you for the pie, dear," she says, beaming at me. "I'll come by to check out the restaurant after the first of the year. I see my family waving me over."

Without another word, she moves past us, pulling her wagon behind and leaving a speechless Ruby in her wake. I watch as she teeters in the snow, smiling as her grown children and small grandchildren close in to embrace her. They all shift towards a bench, pulling the blankets from the wagon and huddling close together as she shows them the pie.

"That was sweet," I murmur, watching the exchange.

Ruby chokes, coughing and sputtering and pounding her chest.

"She thought we were married," she says, words strained as she struggles for breath.

"We make a lovely couple," I say, grinning as she scowls. Then, cocking my head to one side, I study her. "You were worried about me."

Ruby hesitates, eyes flaring.

"I was worried about Christmas," she protests, crossing her arms. "How am I supposed to find the rest of the stars if you're dead?"

I laugh, shaking my head.

"Speaking of stars," I say, and I wince as I lift my closed fist. "I don't know what this is, but we've got to put it somewhere."

"In the bag," she says, dropping her voice to a conspiratorial whisper. With quickness, she opens the small Santa bag at her hip and twists towards me. She nods for me to put the star inside.

Careful not to drop it, I move my hand over the mouth of the bag. Then, only letting her get a glimpse of it, I open my hand and drop the strange, not-quite-solid, not-quite-liquid star into the pouch.

"That's it?" Ruby asks. "That's all we have to do? That doesn't seem so hard."

"Speak for yourself," I retort, snorting. "Next time we find one, I'll let you be the one to catch it."

A smile curls into the corner of her mouth. "How hard could it be? You did it."

"Very hard," I say, trying not to think about what else was very hard before I almost died. If I let my mind venture there again, there's not another hill to throw myself down to escape.

Except, I'm pretty sure Ruby's mind drifts there first.

I watch, stunned into silence, as her face flushes. Her eyes dip down to my lap. They drag back up to my chest. They drop down again. Then, she turns around herself, stroking her hair back and scanning the hill like she's trying to determine our next move.

Did Ruby Warner just check me out and try to hide it?

"Let's look at the map," I say before I let my head get too big.

She looks relieved at my instruction, rather than

irritated, which is another big surprise. I struggle to suppress my smile as she pulls out the map, unfolding it before us. She turns her back to me, coming close so I can look at the map over her shoulder.

"You have to touch," she says, and I swear her voice quivers a little. She almost sounds breathless. "The map. You need to touch the map for it to work."

And work it does as I reach out and take the corner of it. I angle it towards both of us, even though I still can't see the new, glowing star that she seems to see.

"I think it's... moving," Ruby says, turning her head this way and that. "Look, it's turning. It's moving around the square, downtown."

"You think the star is bar hopping?" I tease, looking down at her.

She tilts her head back to look at me, and her red curls catch on the velvet of my vest. She's so close to me, I could bend down and kiss her. She'd probably shove me right into the snow.

"Very funny," she says, unamused. She rolls her eyes and steps away from me, moving towards the hill. "If you beat me to the top, I'll help you clean up your front yard at the end of the night."

She doesn't wait for me to catch up before she starts jogging up the hill. I don't need the extra motivation to follow her, but I do like a challenge. And running up the hill seems far less hazardous than soaring down it on one's stomach. I almost don't notice the way the wooden board landed a foot away from the parking lot. If I'd stayed on it,

I definitely would have hit that truck she'd mentioned. I shudder before I chase after her, biting my tongue so she doesn't catch me smiling.

Ruby Warner just saved me from certain death and asked me to race her up a hill.

And she checked me out.

Maybe this night isn't a complete catastrophe, after all.

SEVEN

RUBY

We're almost to the center of town when Theo grabs the map from the center console. I try to ignore him as he twists it this way and that. In my peripheral, he squints, slowly bringing it closer and closer to his face like it'll make some sort of difference.

"It's not going to work," I mutter under my breath. Based on the way he glares at me, he heard me. "I have to be touching it, and apparently, I'm the only one that can see the stars on the map. You're just some kind of... decoder, or something."

He stares at me in silence long enough that I steal a glance at him. His expression is unreadable, but it's not as rigid as I expected. There's a softness to the set of his brow, and the usual mischievous glint in his eye is absent. Actually, it's a little unsettling how he's looking at me.

"May I?" he asks, extending the map towards me.

At first, I'm not sure what he's asking. Then, his eyes flick towards the exposed inch of skin on my thighs. I shiver, cursing him mentally for reminding me of the cold — *because that's all that shiver was* — and I shrug my shoulders.

He stretches the map across the center of the truck, letting the backside of the paper touch my leg.

"It would just be so helpful if I could see the star," he grumbles, sounding genuinely irritated that he can't be more useful. "You said it was moving around the square?"

I cast a fleeting glance down at the map, pleased to see all the town locations in the correct places. The little, glowing star is still moving in a box around City Hall, and I bite my lip, frowning.

"Maybe it's on a car or something," I murmur, considering. "It could look like a headlight. Perhaps, all the stars are on some sort of light fixture."

"Mmm," he hums, sounding unconvinced. "Where is it — here?"

He points his finger along one street, and the heat of his touch radiates through the paper. My heart stutters, and I open my mouth to tell him to back the hell up, but he's so close to where the actual star has briefly paused that I'm caught off guard.

"No, there," I say, dropping my hand and grabbing his wrist. I move his fingers two inches across the map, trying to ignore the way his fingertips are hovering over my inner thigh. If he wasn't so focused, I'd think this was some sort of perverted ruse to get at me again. "It's paused there. I'm not sure why. We should know in a few seconds though."

I steer the car around a corner, slowing because the

amount of people crowding the streets has increased. There's always a lot happening in town on Christmas Eve, but I thought most people would have made their way to the ice rink by now. I'm not sure why they're still crowding the town center.

"Do you think others can see it?" Theo asks. His head moves back and forth as he studies the map and the crowds of people. "It looks like they're gathering right where it is."

"I hope not," I sigh. This night is already strange enough. We don't need to add any witnesses to it. I'm not sure how to explain knocking Santa off the roof, and I'm still forty percent convinced this is all a dream. There's been too many indications that it's not, though.

I park the truck in an empty spot, surprised that there's one available. Theo hops out, not waiting as I fold up the map and stick it in my pocket. Of course, he doesn't care that I might need help. He's too curious to find out what's happening with the star. He's not responsible enough to remember that we need the map, and he probably hasn't even considered how bad it could be to leave it behind in the truck.

Anything could happen. Anything could go wrong!

My car door opens, and I glance to my left in surprise.

"What are you doing?" I ask, frowning at Theo's outstretched hand.

His brows pull together. "What does it look like I'm doing? I'm helping you out of the truck."

We stare at each other, and I'm waiting for him to make

some sort of off-putting remark about my outfit or my shoes, or call me by another unwanted nickname.

"It's slippery," Theo says, eyes flicking down to the sloshy pavement. "You mentioned earlier that your boots didn't have much traction."

I hesitate, frowning, but I finally twist in my seat, trying to keep my knees together, and I extend my hand towards him.

"Thank you," I say, feeling stiff as he helps me out of the truck.

He's right. It is slippery. The first step seems fine, but when I take another, I almost lose my balance. I grip his forearm with my other hand, and the map slips out of my pocket.

"Woah," he says as my feet slide forward. My lower half slams into him, and my eyes go wide as I tense for the inevitable fall.

He holds me steady though, and a small grin stretches across his face.

"Falling for me already?" he teases, and I realize he has dimples. I don't think I've ever noticed them before.

"There's the Theo Kase I know," I muse, wanting to cut the strange tension between us. I shoot him my best loathsome glare, ready for us to be back to normal. He's been too helpful tonight. Too kind.

I was completely panicked when I realized he could get hurt, and though I never want anyone to get seriously injured on Christmas Eve, I'd be lying to myself if I didn't admit there was a small part of me screaming, *not him,* as he plummeted down the center of Firefly Hill towards certain doom.

Maybe it would have felt like my fault. Maybe it's because I would have had to call the ambulance or the police or the morgue. Maybe it's because I wasn't sure whether the map would work if he wasn't here.

But there was a significant, notable part of me that for some inexplicable reason, knew I would be devastated if that annoying, beautiful, strong man slammed headfirst into a truck and never woke up.

I *liked* seeing Theo across the street.

I would have been disappointed if he didn't have a chance to annoy me one more time in the morning.

My mornings — my life — would have been changed, and I don't like that he suddenly, and unintentionally, has that much of an effect on me and my world.

When did Theo Kase become important to me?

He's still staring at me, and the longer he stares, the longer his words tumble around in my head. *Already falling for me?*

Falling for him?

I scoff, jerking my hands away from him. "You wish, Mr. Kase."

That smile — that stupid, insufferable smile — grows, dammit.

Theo licks his lips, cocking his head. "You hesitated, Red."

"Don't call me that," I snap, no hesitation at all.

He laughs, completely pleased with himself.

"You really did save my life, by the way," he says, stooping to snatch the map off the cold, wet concrete. It looks completely intact despite the way the ink should be dripping. "Thank you for that."

He's standing closer to me when he rises. Somehow, he's ended up barely an inch away.

"The children didn't need to watch you get injured simply because you're an idiot," I retort, straightening my spine. I lift my chin enough that I can almost imagine I'm looking down my nose at him.

His eyes twinkle like he thinks it's cute.

It's not supposed to be cute.

It's supposed to be intimidating.

"Stop diminishing my withering stares," I snap, and I shove my hand against his abdomen hard enough that he stumbles back a step.

He doesn't seem fazed though, and he follows me as I stomp onto the sidewalk, moving towards the gathered crowd near where the star had paused.

It's hard to see around everyone, but there does seem to be some sort of line forming in the chaos. I make my way closer, but it isn't until the crowd turns to look at something else approaching down the perpendicular street that I realize what has drawn so much attention.

"Another horsey, mommy!" a little girl calls, pointing in the distance.

My eyes flick from the road to the parting crowd in front of me, and I find that there really is a horse — or horses. I had no idea the town was doing this, and my mouth pops open in surprise.

Horse drawn carriages are making rounds downtown. Theo catches up to me, muttering something in surprise, but I hardly hear him as a flash of light catches my eye.

"Excuse me!" I call, lifting my hand and waving towards the carriage currently being loaded. A glowing light radiates from the horse's mane where plastic, golden stars are twisted into its hair. Only one of them isn't plastic. It's pure light, calling to me like a flickering flame on a dark night.

An elderly couple pauses, and the driver gives me an irritated look for slowing them down. I grab Theo's wrist and drag him forward, my feet sliding and shifting across the sidewalk.

"Are you tagging in?" the driver asks, frowning at us as we close in on the carriage.

"What?" Theo asks as we slow to a stop. His free hand comes to mine where I have a death grip on his wrist, and he rubs his palm over my fingers. The gesture is intimate, and I yank my hand away as soon as his warmth seeps into me. It's something a boyfriend would do. He lifts a brow in my direction.

"You're late," the driver grumbles, rising to his feet in the carriage. "I was supposed to get a break thirty minutes ago. Here, you can take this one. Better check the rigging, though. I think it's about to come loose."

Without waiting for our reply, he climbs out of the carriage. When he does, I realize instantly why he'd made the assumption. He's also wearing a Santa costume, though his looks much warmer. He hardly looks at either of us as he waves goodbye.

Theo and I exchange glances, but both of our eyes flick to the stars embedded in the horse's mane. Now that we're close enough, I can see that the glowing, magical star looks like it's in some sort of clear container, the light beaming through it proudly. It'll have to be untied — and untangled.

"If you could just give me a second," I say, sending a dazzling smile at the older couple who are eyeing us skeptically.

Theo, to my relief, realizes he needs to stall.

"She's just going to check that everything's secure," he assures the couple, also smiling. Then, he climbs up to the driver's seat and pats the carriage behind him. "Hop on in. This will only take a minute."

I'm not exactly sure what his plan is for once I get the star free. The actual driver is already down the street, heading towards the last few stores that are open. He's doing an awkward jog that makes me realize he probably had to go to the bathroom. No wonder he left so quickly. Everyone's going to be really disappointed when we bolt immediately after getting the star free.

None of them seem to notice the light though. I wonder whether it looks like another regular, plastic star to them.

I circle in front of the horse, not exactly sure whether I'm overstimulating the beast or calming it. It has blinders on, but I want it to know my face before I start pulling on its hair. Surely, that would be better, right?

"Hey, girl," I coo, and I lift my hand to pat its long nose. It has a beautiful cream patch of fur along its snout, and the rest of its coat is thick and brown. I smile, asking, "Or are you a boy? Sorry, I'm not familiar with horses."

"Ruby," Theo hisses from where he sits on the carriage. He nods towards the second carriage pulling up along the street. It slows to a stop, and the horse casually kicks at the ground. "Hurry it up, Red."

"I'm just saying hi," I snap, rolling my eyes at him. I stroke my hand up the center of its face, and it bends its neck, letting me tickle its ears. "Look, it likes me!"

And it's giving me perfect access to the star's container. With its head bowed low, I can reach the ties and clasps if I stand on my toes.

I lean forward, stroking and reaching. My fingers brush the rough, brown string that holds the container in place, and a smile crests my lips.

Then, something terrible happens.

"That's a little too friendly," I scold, shifting to the left as the horse nudges my knees with its big nose. Its lips wiggle, and a long horse tongue tries to lick my boot. I squeal, "Those are new!"

Suddenly, without warning, the creature's massive head bumps against my abdomen. My fingers tighten on its mane just in time as it steps forward, its big nose sliding between my knees. Then, it lifts its head, and I'm airborne.

I scream, grappling and grabbing the horse's coarse mane. There's a terrible snap and a clatter of wood, and my back slams into the massive, wide, fur-covered body.

As it rears up, I realize it's broken free!

"Ruby!" Theo calls.

My eyes fly open, and I see his panicked expression as I cling on for dear life.

"Theo!" I cry out.

Then, the horse lands, and I nearly slip off its side. I manage to hook my foot around it, flipping onto my stomach, and it starts to run.

It gallops down the street at full speed, and I scream, ducking my face against its muscular shoulder. People gasp, and cars honk, and I have no idea where it's going as it tears out of the square and heads towards a wooded area off the side road.

"No, no, no," I protest, looking at the dense trees ahead. "That's going to knock me off!"

I brace myself as it hurtles towards the tree line, and I steal a look over my shoulder, knowing no one is coming to my rescue.

Only, someone is. It's Theo!

Somehow, by some miracle, I'm sure, he's chasing after me on a second horse.

I don't have time to think. I don't have time to question. All I have time for is holding on and hoping I don't fall.

"Ruby!" he bellows, and despite the circumstances, a thrill rolls through me. His horse is faster, and he's gaining on us. There might be hope after all.

The tree line is closing in, and my horse is maintaining a steady, terrifying pace, but my hands are in its mane, my legs are holding tight, and I can almost reach the star.

I grab the small container, and the star bursts with light, radiating out from my hand and spreading in all directions. I give it a tug, trying to tear it free because screw the horse and being gentle with its mane! This thing is trying to kill me!

"Ruby, stay low!" Theo shouts, but I ignore him and lift up a little.

I can't see what I'm doing, and something is caught...

There it is! The strings holding it secure have one little clasp. I reach out, grab it, and unclip it.

"Yes!" I shout, straightening on the horse. I laugh with glee, lifting my arm in victory overhead, but as I do, my horse darts across the last street before the forest.

A car zooms past, blaring its horn, and my horse rears back.

"Ruby!"

My arms windmill, and I shriek. I'm about to eat pavement on Christmas Eve.

My face turns to the sky, I feel myself slipping, and I squeeze my hand tight around the glowing star like it might save me from my fate. I fall, cringing because I know this is going to hurt.

"Oof," a male grunt sounds in my ear.

Strong arms catch me, and I'm cradled to a warm chest as whoever it is stumbles on their feet. They manage to right themselves, and I find myself wrapping my arms around their neck, clinging onto them for dear life.

"I've got you," a low voice promises in my ear, and oh, my gosh it's...

"Theo," I whimper, pulling my face from his shoulder just enough that there's some distance between us. In my periphery, I see his strong neck tensing, his stubble-covered jaw flexing as his chest heaves with exertion. His breath curls in white puffs between us, and despite how much I hate him, I drop my forehead onto his shoulder one more time. "You caught me."

"I couldn't let you fall," he pants, still breathless from the chase. Then, because he's Theo, and he can't even take near-death experiences seriously, he adds with a laugh, "You saved my life, I saved yours. We're even."

I laugh, pressing my face into him because he's warm and despite his muscles, his body is not as hard or as unforgiving as concrete. "How did you do that?"

He chuckles, and his fingers press into where he holds me at my ribs and thighs. "My mom made me take riding lessons with my sister when we were kids. Suzy, my sister, hated it, but I kept it up for a few summers."

"I didn't know you had a sister," I murmur, and my face heats with what feels like embarrassment. I purposefully avoided getting to know this man — I do not like him — but this is the second personal detail I've learned about his life that has me feeling guilty. I hadn't taken the time to consider what family he might have out there, and for some reason, the idea that he has a sister makes me think he might not be quite the womanizer I'd originally thought him to be.

Which could be completely inaccurate. He is a pervert, and he's crude. He could totally be a womanizer.

Still, these little details are humanizing him, and that's guilt that's weighing heavy on my heart.

"Do you have siblings?" Theo asks, still holding me. His voice drops low like we're having an intimate conversation and not recovering from a mad horse-dash through town.

I shake my head, biting my lip, and I turn my face to the side, so I can look up at him with my head on his shoulder. It's the wrong move. It brings us entirely too close together, and Theo blinks at me, looking startled to find my face mere inches from his.

His eyes dip down to my lips.

Slowly, I let my bottom lip slide free, the flesh popping from between my teeth. I'm not sure if I like how he's looking at my mouth, but I don't hate it.

His heaving chest steadies, and the next breath he lets out is heavy and full as heat fills his gaze. I feel his hands flex against me, his fingers stretching as if he could hold more of me, and he lifts his eyes to mine.

"I'm going to put you down now, Ms. Warner."

Something terribly wrong and wild rolls through me. The name I'd so adamantly demanded he call me this morning *does* something to me. It sends a tingle straight down my spine, all the way to my toes, and something tightens low in my belly. Lower than my belly, and oh gosh...

Theo shifts, bending one knee, so he can carefully lower me, feet first, towards the ground. I'm unsteady as my boots touch the concrete, but I'm uncertain whether it's from the rapidly fading adrenaline or the thing that feels a lot like lust that has me squeezing my thighs together.

"Thank you, Mr. Kase," I say, and the pleasure that flashes in his eyes at the sound of his name on my lips as I slide my arms from around his neck is undeniable. It's enough to almost make me forget what I'm holding.

Theo recovers first. He nods towards my glowing hand, and he reaches for the small bag at my hip.

"We should keep that safe," he says, and he tugs the mouth of the bag open.

I drop the star inside, container and all, as a group of concerned witnesses runs up to us.

The world comes crashing back, and I look around with wide eyes. The horse that had taken off with me on its back is strolling along the trees with its head dropped to the snow-covered grass. Theo's horse is drifting along the sidewalk, not wandering very far.

"What have you done?" a man cries out, and it takes a moment to realize it's the man from before who had passed over the duty of carriage driver without further questions. "Ah, my boss would have strangled me!"

"We're going to take a break," Theo says, nodding vaguely. He reaches out and strokes the small of my back with his large hand, the gesture strangely reassuring. He gives me a small pat, cocking his head to one side.

"They're about to light the tree over at the rink," someone in the crowd murmurs, and Theo's head turns in their direction.

Then, he looks at me, eyes softening. "You want to take a break from all this craziness and watch them light the tree?"

I nod, a tremble rolling through me as adrenaline eddies and dissipates.

"Let's go," he says, nodding towards my truck.

I don't protest as he guides me forward. His hand at the small of my back rubs little, soothing circles along my spine.

"Thank you, Theo," I murmur.

His hand only pauses for a second. Then, he resumes his leisurely circles, steering us through the cold night.

EIGHT

THEO

Ruby seems... quiet.

It's not unusual. I'm used to her trying to ignore me. But usually, there's a bite to her quiet. As she drives us towards the ice-skating rink — the one the town sets up in the center of the shopping mall every winter — she seems sad.

"Peppermint for your thoughts," I say, offering her a small, circular mint from a tin in my pocket.

She frowns at it, a line forming between her brows, but when she starts to smile, I know it was the right move.

"It's just starting to seem so real," she admits, taking the mint from me. She pops it into her mouth with a sigh. "You know, when you were flying down that hill, I could still tell myself this was all a dream. But holding onto that horse... My fingers hurt. And my legs feel sore. It's just starting to sink in that I really did kill Santa."

"*We* killed Santa," I amend, and she narrows her eyes at me.

There's that bite.

She holds the steering wheel with her left hand, but her right hand is curled in a fist, resting on her lap.

Did she injure her hand?

Without thinking, I reach out and grab her elbow, guiding her hand over with a gentle tug. It isn't until I'm pulling her glove off that I realize she's allowing it.

I huff, shaking my head. "It kind of makes me regret telling my sister he wasn't real when I was sixteen."

Ruby hisses as I get her last two fingers free, and I pull the material back to find her hand bruised and swollen. My mouth twists as I stare down at her injury. This feels like my fault, somehow. I stroke my thumbs over her palm, wishing I could take away that pain.

"Of course, you told her he wasn't real," she says, rolling her eyes and leaning forward as she drives. "How much older are you than her?"

"Four years," I admit, feeling a little guilty.

She laughs, shaking her head. "That's mean."

"I know," I sigh. "Maybe if I tell her we saved Christmas, she'll finally get over the grudge she's been holding onto. She's been bringing it up for over a decade."

Ruby laughs louder, her head dropping back for a moment. When she grins over at me, her green eyes are gleaming and warm, and there's something like affection shining in her face. Admiration. Interest.

I shift in my seat, straightening up a little.

"I'm sorry about your hand," I say, releasing my hold on her. She pulls it back into her own lap, glancing down once to observe the bruises. "I'll get the next star. No more danger for my Red."

My Red? Did I really just say that?

I train my eyes on the road ahead, relieved for the falling snow flurries, so I can change the subject.

Ruby doesn't bring up the slip of my tongue. I wonder if she even noticed. We fall into easier conversation about the weather as if this is just another, regular night. If it was, though, we wouldn't be here. No, I doubt Ruby Warner would ever willingly be in a car with me if it was any other occasion than saving Christmas. I'm lying to myself — telling myself I'm seeing things that aren't there.

Ruby Warner holds no affection for me. Catching her as she fell off the horse, and her shouting directions as I plummeted downhill towards certain doom, may have softened the night between us, but I have no doubt that the frigid wall of unyielding ice will go right back up in the morning. Our companionship ends with the night. We have one purpose. Resurrect Santa to save Christmas.

As Ruby pulls into the parking lot, I don't ask her what the plan is. Neither of us have mentioned the map, but I saw her glancing at the bag on her hip a few times. I know she's anxious to get this done. She just needs to catch her breath after what happened with the horse. Half an hour at the rink to watch the tree light up isn't going to wreck the rest of the night.

Ruby gets out of the truck before I can help her this time. She cradles her hand close, and I pass her the glove as I fall into step with her. She gives me a tight smile, and we step through the sliding, automatic doors of the mall and into what feels like another universe.

Fake snow is everywhere. Things that are usually drab and plain are covered with glitter. A giant, revolving snow globe displays pricing options and rules for skating, and a neon arrow points the way. We follow it, knowing the tree is going to be at the very center of the rink. Hopefully, it won't take much longer.

We find a spot to sit in some bleachers set up for onlookers and parents who haven't quite stopped their hovering. The rink is clear except for a few people putting garland around the walls, and there, right in the center, is the largest tree I've seen in this small town. I'd thought there were some impressive ones at the festival, but this was something else.

With several ladders around it and decorations scattered across a tree skirt that must be thirty feet across, it's enclosed behind a decorated safety ribbon. It seems like they're almost finished, a few people packing up decorations they must have decided not to use. As we watch, they start to fold up several ladders, but they leave the largest one that goes all the way up to the ceiling rafters, passing the tip of the tree.

"Looks like they're going to put the topper on and light it up," I say, giving her a small grin.

Ruby's face is glowing. Her eyes are soft, her lips curled upwards with affection.

The small crowd we'd followed here is renting skates, and I overhear the person working the counter say they're not letting anyone start skating until the ladders are put up. I shrug my shoulders and look at Ruby.

"We should at least look at the map," Ruby says, and I can tell she's trying to break whatever weird tension she thinks exists between us. More and more people are making their way towards the rink, and the bleachers start to fill up around us as people wait to skate. Ruby pulls out the folded paper from her pocket and leans towards me.

I take one corner, trying to be discreet.

"Oh, my gosh!" Ruby bursts, drawing a few curious glances. She waits until everyone loses interest and leans into me. "There's a star *here.*"

Focus, Theo. Focus.

I try my best to take in the gravity of her words. It's a stroke of luck, but all I can think about is her breath on my neck. She leaned in so close, I swear I felt the brush of her lips against my ear.

I clear my throat and push to my feet, trying to get my mind working again. She stands beside me, and it's nearly impossible not to look at her. She's practically bouncing with excitement. She's shimmying, for Christ's sake.

A glowing light saves my sanity.

"There!" I shout, my voice booming across the frozen space. Ruby jerks in surprise, and she glares at me for drawing attention as a handful of people look our way.

But I don't care. After the night we've had, I'm too relieved. The star — the glowing, magical, taunting bastard — is resting dutifully atop a bin of decorations near the center of the rink, not far from the massive tree. I point it out, ignoring the lingering, curious glances, and Ruby rolls her eyes before following the line of my finger.

"Oh my gosh," she breathes, and I damn near grow three inches at the undeniable awe in her voice. "There's no way it's that easy."

I quickly stride to the entrance to the rink, pausing when I reach the ice. I take a step forward, carefully testing the ice beneath my boot.

"Hiya, guys!"

My foot slides, and I almost eat the wall that encloses the rink, barely catching myself on the corner. I'd been so intent on the star like it was a beacon of hope that I hadn't noticed someone approaching. I glare at the newcomer, but I immediately fix my face when I see it's my neighbor. Or, *our* neighbor.

"Jamison," Ruby says, sounding caught off guard. She takes a step closer to me, bracing her fingers on my elbow like she's trying to hide behind me. "What are you doing here? I thought for sure you'd be at the station. Busy night, right?"

I've never heard her sound nervous like that. I peer over my shoulder at Ruby, taking in the way her cheeks glow with warmth. She tugs at the hem of her dress and crosses her arms over her chest, and the absence of her fingers at the back of my elbow leaves a cold chill.

"Not too busy for holiday cheer," Jamison says, and I slowly drag my attention back to him. He's scanning her up and down — or, at least the parts of her he can see. She's definitely trying to hide behind me. "You two on a date?"

I straighten, shifting in front of her, and I prepare to change the subject. I've never thought much about Jamison, but the way Ruby's energy shifted has me wondering. His blonde hair is perfectly coifed, and his police uniform is spotless. He's always seemed like a decent guy, so why is she shrinking away from him?

"Yes," I say at the same time Ruby says we're, in fact, *not* on a date. A smile automatically screws itself into the corner of my mouth, and I let out a low laugh, shaking my head. I ignore the way Jamison's face lights at her response, and I peer over my shoulder at her, dropping my voice but making sure they can both still hear me. "Come on, Red. Don't tell me you're embarrassed by me."

The smirk I give her is flirty, but I'm trusting she'll understand its purpose is to fend off Jamison. Ruby blinks at me, her head cocking to the side, and her mouth transforms into the perfect pout.

She looks... disappointed.

Does she like this guy?

I think back to the few times I'd recently seen them interact, mostly when they were taking their trash cans out to the curb. She hadn't seemed overly eager to speak with him. But what if she was shy when she liked someone? It would be the complete opposite of how she behaves towards me, but she holds nothing but disdain for me. What if, instead of discomfort, she was just hiding behind me, so he didn't see her in her cute, little Santa dress?

"Just giving you a hard time," I say quickly, nudging her

with my elbow. I lift a brow as I glance at Jamison, studying his reaction.

He looks relieved.

Shit.

"I'm going to see if they need help with the tree," I say, wanting to remove myself from between them as quickly as possible. I go to step on the ice again, hoping I don't fall and look like a complete idiot, but Jamison lifts his hand.

"You need skates to be on the ice," he says, but his eyes are still on Ruby. "They have some rentals over at the counter. It's on me, if Ruby will spare a couple laps around the rink. They won't mind you having early access to the ice if you stay close to me."

He winks.

He can't be serious.

I look at him, and I look at her. There's a disturbing amount of chemistry between them, and I'm suddenly wondering how I've been so blind to it. He's my next-door neighbor. She lives across the street. I've seen them see each other at least once a week.

"A couple laps would be fine," Ruby says, nodding with a sheepish grin on her face.

Something flickers and sinks within me like a single kernel of hope falling into a deep abyss. I started off the day hoping I'd get Ruby to thaw towards me a little, and I think she has. But there was a moment, after I'd caught her when she fell off the horse, where I had a glimpse of what it might be like to have her look at me with something more than tolerance. And I liked it.

I slink behind them as they fall into step with each other, and I pout like an ungrateful child when Jamison passes some skates to me. They go sit on a bench to put on their skates, and they look so nauseatingly perfect together that I squat down right there by the rental counter and shove my skates on, nearly breaking my ankle in my frustration.

I don't wait for them to finish lacing up before I hurtle towards the ice. I'm on the floor and skating towards the tree before anyone can stop me.

Where is it?

Before Jamison had distracted us, the star had been right on top of the box I'm staring at.

I look around, hoping someone placed it with some of the decorations scattered along the tree skirt, but when I glance up, I see it.

Someone had climbed the ladder and left it halfway up the tree.

Well. Looks like this one's not going to be quite so simple.

I start to squat down, awkward on my skates and ready to unlace them. Screw whatever Jamison said about only skates on the ice. Whoever makes the rules can deal with my sock feet sliding to the exit after I grab the star. There's no way I can climb that ladder in skates.

An airy laugh carries through the space, and my gaze shoots up, zeroing in on Ruby despite the growing number lingering near the entrance of the rink.

She's finding her balance as she steps onto the ice,

gripping Jamison's forearms as he skates backwards, leading her. Ruby drops her head back, laughing at something he says, and red spirals of her hair bounce over her shoulders and chest. Her movements seem so effortless, and I bristle, doubting that she needs to hold onto him as tightly as she is.

I straighten my legs, glaring across the ice.

I don't have time to take off my skates. I need to grab the star and get back to her. I need to stop whatever is happening between them because I still need her help to finish what we've started tonight. After I grab this one, we'll have one star left, and I'll be damned if Jamison keeps us from saving Christmas.

I turn, moving my feet sporadically as I try to keep them under me. Then, I step onto the tree skirt because no one else is here to tell me I shouldn't. The ladder isn't that far. This can't be that hard.

When I reach it, I check that it's secure. It seems mostly stable. I grip the sides and take my first step up, bracing the blade of my skate into the corner of the step.

There. That seems remarkable stable, actually. Nothing could go wrong.

I start my way up, almost laughing at how easy it is. As long as I don't shift my weight too far forward or too far back, it's perfectly fine. I just need to go up and down.

I count down the rungs of the ladder as I approach the glowing light. Ten, nine… Five…

"Gotcha," I say, snatching the little monster in one fist. It flickers, burning brighter between my clenched fingers.

"Let's get you into the bag."

I peer over at Ruby and notice that she's still following Jamison.

No. Not following.

Touching.

Her hand is stroking his bicep up and down like she's trying to stroke something else, and he's definitely flexing.

"What the…"

I grip the star tighter, not wanting to lose it on my trek back down the ladder. There's a couple of other people still decorating the tree, but none of them have complained that I'm up here.

I step down once, and a quiet sound makes my heart stop.

Was that metal? I look at the tree, sure the branches just shook.

I hear a small scream, and a girl who'd been adjusting something near the bottom of the tree takes off running. "It's coming down!"

Coming down?

Others scatter, but I look at Ruby. She's just far enough away with Jamison that they didn't hear the girl's warning, but they're close enough that the tree could fall on them.

It starts to lean in their direction.

"Ruby!" I bellow.

She frowns, turning her attention to me.

There's no time to warn her. In her skates, she looks like a baby deer trying to stand still for the first time, and Jamison looks frozen.

This is going to hurt.

I shove the star into my vest pocket, hoping it stays put, and I grip the sides of the massive ladder with both hands. Without taking time to think it through, the tree shifting slowly next to me, I jump my feet out, bracing my skates against the sides of the ladder, and I slide.

I am like a freaking superhero. I don't even break my ankles when I land.

The tree is definitely falling, and Jamison looks green, and Ruby is gloriously red, and I take off for her. I'm glad I do because Jamison, the jerk, shifts away from her with a look of horror.

He's actually going to leave her there.

"I'm coming, Ruby!" I roar, and I skate full speed ahead across the ice as if it's something I've practiced every day of my life. Adrenaline is kicking in, and Ruby's eyes float upwards behind me. The shadow of the tree looms over us on the ice, and I'm not sure how far over it has tipped by the time I reach her.

All I know is we're about to go down.

I grab her, twisting and turning to try to lessen the impact, and I do my best to move us out of harm's way. But I have not skated every day of my life — I've barely skated at all — and I lose my balance before we're completely out of the tree's path.

We hit the ice, and I hold onto her, relieved she's mostly on top of me. Then, we're covered in green and glittering red and gold, the tree enveloping us.

I squeeze my eyes shut, curling my arms around her as

if I could protect her. It isn't until everything has stopped moving that I realize she's curled around me too. And we're okay.

Ruby breathes heavily, trembling against me.

"Ruby?" I ask, panting. My arms shake around her, and her fists grip the front of my vest.

"We're okay," she whispers.

I drop my head back with relief, not minding the dull pain when it hits the ice a little too hard. We're surrounded by lights and glittering glass bulbs and other ornaments, and I swallow thickly.

Then, I feel her thighs squeeze my hips as she tries to push herself upright.

She's straddling me?

God, why is that my biggest concern right now? We were almost crushed by a tree!

Still, I know she's wearing a very short skirt, and though the tree seems to be mostly covering us, I don't want anyone — especially that coward, Jamison — seeing her exposed. I bend my knees up, hoping to shield her, but it only causes my thighs to brush against her rear.

Ruby falls forward, gasping as she barely catches herself, her palms against the ice just over my head.

"Why'd you do that?" she hisses.

I can feel her glaring down at me, but I squeeze my eyes shut because now, directly in front of my face, are two very enticing things that should not be that close to my mouth.

"I was trying to help," I groan, feeling her shift against my thighs. I pinch my eyes tighter, trying to clear my head, but the heat of her is all around me, and she smells so fucking good. "I'm not looking. Just stand up."

"I can't," she snaps, and I feel her moving against my thighs again. She pushes back, and I feel her weight come down on my lap, and...

Oh no. Not again.

"Ruby."

"Something is wrapped around my legs," she says, irritated.

She's so irritated that she hasn't noticed the problem growing between us. A problem I seem to have no control over despite how many morbid things I try to force into my brain.

That's okay. I'll just slide out from beneath her.

I start to move, groaning as I slide on the ice. There's a rattle of tree branches and ornaments fall, and Ruby cries out in pain.

"Stop!" She shouts, her legs squeezing around me. "Stop, don't move! Something's pulling my hair."

It's the worst possible thing I can do, but I open my eyes. I immediately regret it as all the blood drains down my body, flowing to one central point.

"Ruby," I try again, wanting to get her attention without alarming her.

She's sitting perfectly upright, tree branches framing her waist as she twists between them. A string of lights is tangled with her hair, pulling her head back, leaving her neck arched and exposed.

She looks so fucking beautiful with her body straining

like that, and she's sitting right on top of my swelling cock. She reaches for her hair, trying to undo it, but it must be hurting her because she shifts against me, whimpering.

"Ruby, please," I beg, my voice almost failing me.

"I'm not that heavy," she whines, and dammit, she sounds like she's in pain.

I watch as she struggles to free herself, and I try to pay attention to what her hands are doing with the lights instead of the part of her that's grinding against my pants with every small movement she makes. She thinks I want her off me because she's too heavy, and she doesn't know that my entire body is just begging her to sit down harder.

"There!" She gasps, and tree branches snap with loosened tension, adjusting around her as she looks down at me. "What's wrong?"

"I just need you to get off of me," I say, trying to spare her from the mortifying truth. She already thinks I'm deplorable. She doesn't need to know I'm a total pig.

"Are you serious?" she asks, her irritation clear. "This is your fault."

She reaches back to try to free her legs again.

"It is my fault, yes," I admit, closing my eyes again. I'm not sure how this exact predicament is my fault, but I'm sure karma put me here. Her pelvis moves forward, and there's no way she doesn't feel that. "I'm sorry."

I can feel her body stiffen, and I don't need to open my eyes to feel the heat of her searing glare.

"Are you getting off on this?" she asks, disgust clear in her voice. "You can't be serious."

"Ruby, please, just —"

"Not a problem," she snaps, and she tries to push herself off me.

Only her legs aren't free, and the tree moves in response to her tugging. A branch snaps free from where it'd been restrained, swinging over her head. She barely ducks in time, but it's still not fast enough. Her hair is safe, but this time, it's so much worse.

"No!" She squeals, barely catching herself with her hands over my head. The tree branch hooked onto part of her dress, pulling her forward, so she's completely sprawled on top of me. "Theo, I'm sorry!"

Sorry? She's sorry?

This would be the hottest thing anyone's ever done for me if it was completely consensual.

Her breasts are smashed into my face, and I'm doing everything I can to pretend they're not there, but in her panic, she won't stop moving.

Ruby wriggles, and…

Oh. My. God.

"Theo, my ass is out," she whisper-hisses, panic coursing through her body.

The low murmur of other people is building, and I realize, with horror, that people are coming to help us. They're probably hoping we're not dead.

"Theo, my ass!"

"Fuck it," I growl, my words muffled by her breasts. I bend my knees up higher, assuring that she's shielded from view, but she plops down hard. I groan, unable to stop myself from dragging my face to one side. Her breast feels so fucking bitable.

"Oh, Theo," She whispers, my name coming out of her mouth like a desperate plea. She shifts, her boob sliding over my mouth, and she manages to twist just enough that I can turn my face and be free of temptation. "Theo, I'm sorry."

Ruby manages to move both hands to one side of me, so she's at least angled onto my shoulder instead of my face. It's enough freedom that I can look down, and I brace my hands on her hips, trying to get a better view of what she's tangled in.

The sight is dizzying. Her dress has ridden up just enough that only the white fur trim shields her panties from view. I groan, my hips rising automatically, and this fucking woman shudders on top of me.

"Theo," she moans, and it's undeniable that her hips rock forward, riding out my movement.

"Ruby, stop," I plead, even as my hips move automatically, grinding me into her.

"I'm so sorry," she sighs, shutting her eyes. Her cheeks turn pink, and I feel her thighs tighten around me as she shudders again. "I can't help it. You're the one moving, and it feels good. It feels so good, Theo."

She's going to kill me. I'm going to die in the middle of the ice rink with jizz in my pants and Ruby's pussy warming my lap.

"You're going to make me come," I hiss, dropping my voice in warning. "Stop that. People are walking this way."

"I'm going to come," she whispers. And then she pleads with me, so sweetly, that Jesus fucking Christ himself couldn't forgive my next sins. "I need to come, Theo. Please. I'm so sorry."

I grip her hips to hold her still, trying to stop whatever is happening right now, but I can feel her clench on top of me, and there's an undeniable sound of pleasure that squeaks from her.

I explode inside my Santa pants, groaning and moving her atop me, grinding her into me because damn, she's enjoying it. Her sounds are muffled, and I think she's covering her mouth, but she's moving her hips too, pressing down as I drag her forward and back against me.

She's coming apart on top of me, and I'm making sure she enjoys every last second of it because I'm definitely going to hell for this.

We're left panting and immobile, Ruby draped across me as people finally come into view. The only redeeming part about what I've just done is that my legs are still mostly blocking her from view, protecting whatever modesty she has left.

What the hell just happened?

What the hell did I just do?

This is so much worse than killing Santa.

She'll never forgive me after this. I'm pretty sure I just made us both orgasm after multiple near-death experiences.

"I'm glad you two are alright!" says a cheery voice. Some woman comes into view, and she stoops to untangle

Ruby's legs finally. "We were so worried! That tree came down, and we all thought it was lights out for the two of you! That was like a Christmas miracle!"

"Yeah, a miracle," I say bitterly.

I wait as they free Ruby first, helping her climb through the branches and make her way out of the tree. I help myself out, pushing to my feet and trailing after her, watching how shaky she is on her legs.

I doubt it's from the tree or the skates. That's pleasure making her unsteady, and her cheeks are red when she turns to look at me.

"Did you get it?" she asks as soon as we lose everyone's attention.

"Yeah," I say, nodding my head. I pat my vest where the star is resting safely in my pocket. "Let's get some air."

Then, without waiting for her permission or agreement, I skate off the rink and tear of my skates, only staying long enough to lace up my boots before I push out the doors and into the frigid air.

NINE

RUBY

"So, that was interesting," I say, trying to find a way to move forward from what happened twenty-seven minutes ago.

Theo hasn't said a word since we left the ice rink. We left my car at the mall and walked until we came upon some winding trails of Christmas lights. He put the third star in the pouch at my hip, and we've been walking through the beautifully lit paths in silence.

And what did I expect to happen?

Nothing. Because that wasn't planned.

Theo and I both fell apart at the seams, and I had the most mind-blowing orgasm I've ever had in the middle of the shopping mall.

And I just said it was *interesting*.

"You know, it's really not a big deal," I try again, needing him to say *something*. "If anything, we can blame it on the stress of tonight."

Theo looks away, but not before I catch his face twist

with agitation. His shoulders bunch, and he blows out a heavy breath, frosted air curling before him. "Can we not talk about it?"

There. Six words. That's something, right?

I sigh in relief because it feels like a victory compared to the silence. I try to ignore how defeated he sounds, and I move closer to him to match his long stride.

"Thank you for trying to rescue me from Jamison," I say, shifting the subject to something else. I'm not sure why, but I feel like everything that happened in the tree was my fault, and I need to level the playing field. "We went out a few years ago — on just *one* date. He's actually much more insufferable than you."

Theo's head snaps around. His brows pinch together, and he looks at me with those blue eyes. When the light hits them just right, green lines gleam like shards of emerald in his irises. It's enough to steal my breath, and I almost forget what I just admitted to him.

"You're not interested in him?" Theo asks, maintaining eye contact. He looks so serious as if the rest of the night teeters on uncertainty as he awaits my answer.

"In Jamison?" I ask.

He can't be serious.

"He was rude to our waitress, and my Aunt Maddy never liked him. I can't go out with someone my aunt didn't like. She said he only ever spoke to her if I was there to witness it."

Theo's frown deepens, a line forming between his brows, but he drops his gaze to the gravel path beneath our feet as we continue forward, his pace slowing.

"Your aunt, huh," he says as if mulling over a thought. "The same aunt you mentioned earlier? The one that would take you sledding down Death Hill with your uncle?"

I can't stop the laugh that bursts from me, and Theo's responding smile is immediate and wide.

"Yes, the one and only," I say, grinning as I remember her. "This time of year, she'd always style her hair into a low bun and bustle around like Mrs. Claus herself."

"You and Christmas," Theo chuckles, shaking his head. "Are they coming to visit? Maybe we can put our feud to rest if they don't hate me too much."

It's been long enough that the sorrow doesn't cut so deep. If anything, the Santa disaster after the festival numbed me to their absence. Uncle Joe would have never let Santa on the roof in the first place.

"They passed away a few years ago," I admit, the words coming easier than the last few times I'd said them. "They raised me, so all the family holiday traditions came from them. Participating in the winter festival, decorating the house, the restaurant, the hot chocolate recipe. Now, it's all up to me."

"Oh," Theo mutters, dropping his gaze. He stops abruptly, staring at the path beneath his feet. "So earlier, when you said I wrecked your Christmas and stole hot chocolate... That was about them?"

Silence hovers between us, but I give him a small nod. "You didn't know."

Theo lets out a heavy sigh, stuffing his hands in his pockets. He tilts his head, studying me. "My mom was an only child, and she moved us to the city after our grandparents died. Never really knew my dad. So, this is my first Christmas without my mom and my sister. I invited them to come, but they're busy with work. They're coming for New Years, though. And I know they'd like you."

I can't stop the small smile from crooking in the corner of my mouth. "Really? Me? The girl who left a chocolate penis in your front yard."

"Well, they are very against littering, but I can keep that instance between us," Theo says, laughing. He presses his lips together, and something about his expression changes. Softens. Shifts like the energy between us.

"Thank you," I say, shifting on my feet. Somehow, he's gotten so close to me, and our breath mingles between us, the clouds of white mixing between our bodies.

"Could you keep that other instance between us?" Theo asks, his voice dipping low. "The one where I first saw you dressed in red. My mom might honestly skin me alive for that. I swear, I never meant any harm. I thought you were coming onto me."

It's the first time he's directly admitted that there was miscommunication. Every other time we've broached the subject of *the incident,* he's made some sort of perverted remark or joke, or invented some new nickname.

My throat tightens, and I know my eyes are wide as I get lost in my thoughts, stumbling around for what to say.

This man has seen me in lingerie. He's touched me in lingerie. He came undone between my thighs half an hour ago while I shattered on top of him, and he's looking at me earnestly as if he truly wants to bury whatever bloody hatchet I'd been wielding defensively between us.

"You make the best cookies I've ever had, which is saying a lot," Theo admits, his voice low and grumbly. "I've been trying to think of ways to thank you ever since, but it seems I prefer to torment. Maybe that's why karma is eating me tonight."

"You think spending time with me is punishment?" I ask, taken aback. I can't help but notice how disappointed I sound.

"No," he says quickly. "But it was pretty damn humiliating coming prematurely like a teenager because you wouldn't stop wriggling on top of me."

Heat immediately licks at my cheeks, and I drop my gaze.

Fingers, warm and soft, stroke across my jaw, and Theo lifts my face, so I'm looking at him.

"I promise you, Red," he murmurs, his voice gruff, "I never meant for anything bad to happen between us. You're the most remarkable person I've had the pleasure of meeting, and you're a beautiful woman. Any time with you is a blessing. I'm just *your* curse."

He chuckles, low and deep with his last words. He's so close to me, and I'm going limp for him. I lean into him, letting him hold me as we peer into each other's eyes, his free hand finding my lower back.

"I don't think you're a curse," I whisper, letting him tilt my chin up.

That's when I notice it.

The glow above his head, dancing in the branches of the tree.

"Theo," I breathe, and his hand slides along my jaw, his fingers slipping into my hair. "The star."

Theo freezes, and his eyes dance back and forth between mine. He notes the way my attention has shifted, and his hands fall away. He looks up, huffing out a breath.

"That's the last one," he says, and he reaches up to take it. He hardly looks at me as he loosens the bag at my hip, and he puts it inside. Then, a phone rings, and it takes me a second to realize it's his, stashed in one of his pockets. "I'll be right back, Red."

The night is cold as he walks away, lifting his phone to his ear as he leaves me on the glowing path. Confusion swirls inside me, and disappointment is bitter and biting.

Was Theo about to kiss me?

I wanted Theo to kiss me.

I'm not sure how to digest these feelings, so I turn and stroll a few paces in the opposite direction, not wanting to stray too far. I wrap my arms around myself, wondering what we're supposed to do next with the bag of stars, but a familiar face comes into view as someone rounds the corner.

It's Jamison. Again.

"Ruby!" he calls, waving an arm overhead. "I'm glad to find you! I was so worried when you left the rink so quickly. I wanted to check on you.”

“I’m fine,” I assure him, giving him a smile, and he continues towards me.

“Good!” he says. “What happened to your, uh… date? He run off and leave you?”

It takes everything in me not to point out that running off and leaving me is exactly what Jamison did on the ice rink, but I look over my shoulder, about to point Theo out. Before I get a chance to, Jamison closes the distance between us, and I step back in alarm.

“Look above you, Ruby,” he says, smiling enthusiastically. “Mistletoe!”

It’s true. Mistletoe hangs low from a branch, decorated with lights and glitter. Someone had hung it there, and I stopped directly under it.

“May I?” Jamison asks.

He starts to lean in without waiting for my answer.

“Uhh…”

I have no idea what to do in this situation. This is about to be really awkward.

“I’m back,” a deep voice says from behind me.

Relief sweeps through me, and my eyes widen at the sound of Theo’s voice. I’m about to turn towards him, but a strong, gentle hand grips my shoulder.

“No need, Jamison,” Theo says, the warning clear in his voice. “Ruby’s with me tonight.”

Theo turns me towards him, and before I can even thank him, his hands cup my face. He closes his mouth over mine, stealing my breath and taking my lips and claiming my mind.

My senses go wild.

Theo tastes like peppermint and smells like pine, and he feels so warm as he saves me for the third time. He holds me steady which is a relief because my head is spinning as I open for him. His tongue slides against mine, and I moan. The sound only urges him to do more, and his hands find my waist. He tugs my body against his, holding me and touching me and kissing me in a way that no one ever has.

He kisses me like it's the best thing in the world, and he's been waiting to do it.

He kisses me like I'm already his. Like he knows I need him to kiss me in this exact, perfect way.

I'm breathing hard when we slowly break apart. I open my eyes, my vision swimming as I search for him.

He stares down at me, his chest rising and falling with mine. He studies my face like he's memorizing this moment. Memorizing me.

"Mistletoe," I whisper, and I search his gaze for an answer to some question I can't form.

Theo falters. Then, he looks up, spotting the mistletoe in the tree.

Did he not know it was there?

"Let's figure out what to do with the stars," Theo says, putting up his guard.

He doesn't say anything about the mistletoe as he slips his arm around me and steers me away from the vacant place Jamison had vanished from.

TEN

THEO

Ruby doesn't say anything.

I thought being too embarrassed to talk after coming in my pants would be the low part of my evening, but now I feel like a complete asshole.

Ruby needed help. That much was clear. I had no idea why Jamison thought he could kiss her — I didn't see the mistletoe — and all I knew was that I had to stop it.

But instead of interrupting, I stole a kiss for myself.

Spontaneous kisses aren't cute in real life. They're only cute in movies, or when you know, without a doubt, that the other person wants you to kiss them.

Ruby didn't want me to kiss her.

She couldn't have.

She allowed it because of the mistletoe.

There was a moment when I thought she was kissing me back, but now, her silence speaks volumes.

She absolutely hates me for what I just did, and there's no taking it back.

Suddenly, she breaks her silence and asks, "Why aren't you saying anything?"

She turns just enough to look me over, and her expression is guarded and weary.

I'm not sure why I haven't tried to break the silence between us. I thought I'd be nice for once and let her simmer in her rage instead of poking the bear. "What do you want me to say?"

Really? What does she want me to say?

I know exactly what I should say. I should say sorry. I should apologize. I should grovel at her feet, so we can move past this moment and get on with the night instead of aimlessly walking back through the paths of lights.

Ruby frowns, staring at her feet as she walks. I watch out of the corner of my eye as her shoulders curl forward, and the sight of her shrinking breaks my heart.

I can't stand it anymore.

I take hold of her elbow, gentle but urgent, and I guide her over to the side of the path, so people can walk past us.

"Ruby, I'm so sorry," I start, shaking my head. "I saw you talking with Jamison again, and all I could think about was how he left you on the ice rink when that tree was falling. It looked like he was about to kiss you, and I didn't see the mistletoe, and I just… couldn't. I couldn't let him kiss you. Not without some sort of redemption for earlier. I would rather you hate me completely than watch you settle for some jerk who hides his cowardice behind a badge. And you said your aunt hated him."

Ruby stares vacantly at the space between us. Then, she slowly lifts her gaze, her green eyes gleaming, and I'm not sure whether her eyes are stinging from the cold or if she's about to cry.

"You thought kissing me would make me hate you," she says, but she sounds confused. Her left eyebrow arches as her head cocks a little to the side, and I don't know what possesses me, but I lift my hand.

I stroke her cheek and push her hair behind her ear, letting my fingers linger in the coppery tendrils. "It was a risk I was willing to take."

She frowns, a line forming between her brows, and she drops her gaze.

"I don't hate you, Theo," she says, so quietly, I almost can't make out her words. "I didn't want to kiss Jamison. Thank you… For helping me."

I stare at her so long, not believing I heard her correctly.

Finally, I clear my throat. "You're welcome. It was my pleasure."

Okay, that's too much. I groan internally at my inability to keep my mouth shut.

Ruby's eyes flick to mine, and it might be my imagination, but I think there's a small smile playing on her lips. I swear the corner of her mouth tugs upwards.

A siren cuts through the night, interrupting the moment and instantly shattering the tension I hadn't realized was building.

"Theo?" Ruby asks, concern emanating from her body as she looks past my shoulder. She points, shock and disbelief etching her face.

I turn to see what she's seeing.

Up on the hill, away from the trails and along one of the quiet, side streets that leads to a neighborhood, are five police cars, which seems excessive for the size of the town. The night must have been boring them. What could they…

No.

No, it can't be!

"He's supposed to be dead!" I burst, staring in disbelief. "He went poof and turned into snow fluff. That can't be him!"

"It's definitely him," Ruby wails in disbelief. She leans into me, and in her despair, she actually braces her hands against my chest. I don't question it. I just wrap my arm around her. "What did he do?"

Up on the hill, Santa — the real Santa — is getting arrested. We're close enough, his face is easy to make out in the glowing streetlights. He smiles and laughs cheerily as Jamison — of all people — puts handcuffs on him.

"It doesn't matter what he did," I grumble, shaking my head. I rub a small circle on Ruby's back, hoping it's comforting. "How are we supposed to get the bag of stars to him now?"

"I could be a distraction."

Her voice is breathy, and her eyes are wide, and before I can comprehend her suggestion, she tugs at her dress. She adjusts the top part, so her breasts are more exposed, and she hikes up her skirt a little.

"Please, don't let this be for nothing," she says, and she takes off before I can stop her.

"Ruby!" I hiss, but it's too late.

She charges through the snow in her boots, moving up the hill. The cops aren't that far away, and Jamison is patiently waiting for Santa to finish whatever he's saying, not moving him towards a car yet.

Halfway up the hill, Ruby lets out a shriek, throws her arms into the air, and calls out, "Jamison! Help me!"

Like a true damsel, she collapses into the snow, rolling several feet down the hill.

Shit.

I take off uphill, moving through the trees a good distance away while trying to keep my eyes on her. Her plan works like a charm, though. Jamison immediately abandons Santa, leaving him unattended, as all the cops run down the hill to assist.

Ruby makes a scene of rolling in the snow, tossing her arms dramatically. Her skirt rides up, and I know she must be freezing because the skin of her thighs is already bright pink and starting to turn red. I can almost see her ass, but I can't worry about that this time.

I have to get to Santa. Ruby will be pissed if I let this moment get wasted.

"Santa," I hiss, rushing towards him as Ruby's dramatic cries carry through the night. A quick glance down the hill, and I see she's still making a scene of tumbling away, rolling out of reach every time someone's about to save her.

"Oh my gosh," she calls out, her voice high and comical. "Jamison, help me, please!"

"I hate him," I hiss, shaking my head. "I hate that guy so much right now."

Santa chuckles, clearly amused. "You'll hate him less when I tell you he left his keys on the seat."

Oh, that stupid bastard.

"Thanks," I whisper, grabbing the keys. I make quick work of freeing Santa. Then, we both turn and look down the hill.

Ruby is being helped to her feet by an older man, and most of the cops are scratching their heads, clearly wondering why she just did all that. Jamison seems convinced she needed a hero, but most of them are looking at her like she's some kind of idiot who just wants his attention.

If only they knew how little of his attention she wanted.

"All I need is that bag on her hip, and I'll be ready to go," Santa says, bouncing on his heels. "My sleigh is just through those trees over there. You've got about five minutes before it's too late."

I turn to look at Santa — and he's gone.

Turning around myself, I scan the trees, trying to figure out which ones he meant. I hear something jingle, and a gleam of red and gold catches my eye.

Bingo.

I start to call out to her, but I can't let anyone realize what I've just done. I rush down the hill, taking the same path through the trees that I'd run up. Then, I take a loop along the far path, coming up from the opposite direction.

"Ruby!" I call, rushing towards her.

She's in Jamison's arms, pretending like she's about to faint.

"Oh, man," I say, moving in. I force my way between them, taking her in one arm while patting him on the shoulder. "You really saved the day, Jamison. I don't know how to thank you. I went to get the truck, but I heard her screaming."

Jamison looks between us warily and says, "I'll let you take it from here. Just get her home safely."

His words are both a surprise and a relief. I try not to seem too excited as the cops all slowly move back up the hill. I squeeze Ruby's waist gently, turning her away, so we don't have to witness them realizing that Santa is missing.

"We just have to give him the bag," I say, leaning down to whisper in her ear. "He's in the trees on the other side of the hill. We only have a couple minutes."

Finding Santa is easy. Giving him the bag is a relief. Seeing the reindeer is alarming.

Ruby and I keep a safe distance, wondering how the massive creatures made it into the trees without being noticed.

"Can those actually fly?" Ruby asks, taking a step into me.

Santa chuckles, shaking his head in amusement.

"The two of you seem to be getting along much better," he says, smiling proudly. "Might I suggest getting each other home safely? I have a lot of presents to deliver. No one else can see me, but your gawking might give me away."

He laughs again, his entire body shaking like it's the funniest thing he's ever said.

Ruby and I step back, watching him climb onto his sleigh. There are nine reindeer — none with red noses. I want to see what happens, but Santa gives us a stern look, crossing his wrists while he takes the reins.

"I'm waiting," he says, shooing us with a flick of his wrist.

"Oh," Ruby says, bouncing like she's startled. "Okay. Bye then."

She turns stiffly, elbowing me in the ribs to do the same.

We make it three steps when we hear a whoosh and a jingle. When we turn around, Santa, the reindeer, and his sleigh are gone.

"Is this real?" Ruby asks, her voice small. She loops her arm around my waist, turning towards me, and her touch is everything I've been waiting for.

I peer down at her, studying her face. "Yeah, Red. It's all real."

She holds my gaze. "If this is a dream, let me stay in it a little longer."

I assured her that she wasn't dreaming. I promised it was real as I walked her to her door. I told her I would remind her tomorrow that it all happened, so she had no doubts, and I almost kissed her goodnight.

I stand in my entryway, just inside my front door, for

five minutes, rethinking that almost-kiss.

I should have kissed her.

I take one step further into my dark house, disappointed with myself, and a knock sounds on my door.

I turn around so fast, I almost trip on my rug. Ruby's silhouette is clear through the shaded window next to my front door, the porch light shining down on her. I pull the door open, stunned that she's standing there.

"Can we do something normal?" she asks. She lifts a basket in front of herself, and it's filled with cookies, popcorn, and several DVDs. There's also a small, black box, and it takes me a few minutes to realize it's a DVD player.

"You seem prepared," I say, pushing my front door open as I step aside.

As she walks into my home, it's like she brings joy inside with her. The darkness doesn't seem so empty, and I guide her forward, turning on lamps as I lead her to my living room.

"I'm glad you brought a player. I don't use DVDs."

"I thought you might be a digital guy," she says, smiling. She puts the basket on the coffee table and hands me a bag of microwave popcorn. "I'll hook it up while you handle this?"

I smile widely, surprised by how much relief she's given me just by being here.

"We should have done this a long time ago," I admit. Then, because it's freezing in my house, I add, "I'll get some blankets, too."

We watch *Home Alone,* which is surprising because I didn't even know you could get that movie as a DVD. I remember having it on VHS back when I was a kid, and it feels good to laugh.

It feels even better to sit with Ruby, my arm stretched on the couch behind her while we share a blanket. Halfway through the movie, she puts her head on my chest and her palm against my stomach, and by the end of it, we're lying down.

She doesn't seem uncomfortable, resting atop me. It feels like the most natural thing in the world as I run my fingers across her back and play with her hair. If she hadn't laughed so many times, I would have thought she'd fallen asleep.

"I should go," Ruby murmurs long after the credits have ended.

She doesn't have to. I'd be happy to have her here all night, just like this.

"I'll walk you back," I offer, and I try not to seem disappointed when she climbs off me.

We walk slowly through my house. She came over in pajamas, and I'd changed into sweats while we were getting ready for the movie. Still, when we open that front door, the cold air feels biting.

Ruby turns to face me, stopping me from walking her across the street.

"Theo," she says, her voice taking on a kind of urgency as her eyes flick between mine. It's such a sudden change from how relaxed she was a moment ago, and my spine straightens, concern rolling through me.

"What is it, Red?" I ask.

She smiles at the nickname, standing in my doorway, the cold world at her back.

"I'm going to be really disappointed if you don't kiss me under your own mistletoe."

I blink. Then I look at the small patch of greenery hanging over my door. Honestly, I'd forgotten I'd put it there.

"You want me to kiss you, Red?"

Ruby bites her lip, blushing, but she nods. "Only if you want to."

Only if I want to? She has to be out of her mind if she thinks I'd let a chance to kiss her pass me by, again, tonight.

"I should have brought out the mistletoe this summer," I tease. Then, I close the distance between us and kiss her.

ELEVEN

RUBY

When Theo kisses me, it's nothing like the way he kissed me before.

The first time, he'd been commanding and desperate, and all I could do was try to stand upright as I got swept away in the feel of his lips on mine, the taste of his tongue.

This time, I had time to think about it. I thought about it through the entire second half of the movie, and I was surprised he didn't make a move while I was curled against his chest, shifting my legs against his when I wanted more warmth.

And I was so nervous. I could barely get the words out, but he seemed so sincere about not wanting to wreck my Christmas. If I'd walked across the street to my empty house, unkissed, Christmas would have been fine, but I would have been a wreck. I would have thought about it the rest of the night, unable to sleep, and it would have consumed my thoughts Christmas Day.

Theo's mouth moves over mine, his tongue sweeping

in, and I wrap my arms around his neck. His hands slide across my waist, and his fists clench the fabric of my pajama sweater. I press myself against him, wanting more, but I can feel him holding back.

I drag my hands down his chest to press my palms into his abdomen, his soft shirt making it easy to navigate the contours of his torso.

"Ruby, wait," he groans, turning his face to the side. He dips his head and kisses my shoulder, and his hands at my waist rub up and down, his thumbs tickling my ribs. "If you do that, I'm not going to walk you across the street."

I bite my lip, melting into the heat of his breath against my neck. "Then, invite me back inside. It's so cold out here."

A low chuckle rises from his chest, and I feel the vibrations of it go straight to my core. I bite back the whimper fighting to get out as I turn my face to his. I kiss his cheek.

"Ruby, I —"

"Red."

His hands stop moving, and his chest stops rising. "What?"

Heart thundering, I steel my nerves. "I want you to call me Red."

I kiss his cheek again, almost shuddering as he turns his face towards mine, and the corner of his mouth twists with delight.

"Okay, Red," he growls, his voice dropping an octave. He clears his throat and pulls away enough that he can look down at me. He cups my face with one hand, his fingers brushing back my hair. "I'm not sure if you know what you're asking for. I might not have the best intentions if I take you inside."

He thinks he has the upper hand. He's riled me up all year, and he thinks I'm some sweet, innocent girl because I grew up in this tiny town.

Did he already forget what happened while we were tangled in that giant tree at the ice rink? Does he really think someone completely innocent would buy the lingerie he caught me in?

I press my fingers into his stomach where they've been resting on the lower V of his abdomen, and I rise on my toes, bringing my lips to his ear. "I came over here without the best intentions, Mr. Kase. Can you not tell what's under that sweater you're clutching so tightly?"

Something pulses against my lap, and I smile against his ear. *That* got his attention.

"You're in pajamas," he says flatly, but he doesn't move an inch. "You brought popcorn and family movies, and you had a really long night."

I sigh into his ear, slowly dragging my hands back up his body. I press my chest against his as I coil my arms around his neck, and I pull back to look at him, arching a brow. "Are you really going to turn me down on Christmas?"

There it is. I threw myself out there, and now, I'm just hoping that after all we've been through together, he'll catch me to keep me from feeling like a perverted jerk.

Theo's fingers tighten in my sweater. Then, he peers down as he shifts his fist up.

I know the moment he catches a hint of something bright red because his eyes darken, and his gentle, patient face sharpens with severe focus. His hand that had so sweetly swept back my hair before finding its way to hover over my back, flattens, his fingertips tracing my spine.

"Red," he says, and there's a note of amusement in his voice. "Is that what I think it is?"

He peels his eyes away from the hint of fabric, and when his gaze meets mine, it's smothering. I can hardly breathe as his eyes bore into mine, reading me so easily.

A grin stretches across Theo's face, and he slowly shakes his head, tsking. "Oh, Red. No wonder you made the naughty list with me."

"Just trying to keep you from taking that spot at the top," I tease, smiling sweetly.

Theo stares at me for several seconds. Then, he kicks his front door open wider and pulls me over the threshold. He shuts the door quickly, backing me against it, and I'm ready for him to kiss me — to take me — but he braces his palms against the wood, framing my head.

My heart thunders, and my nerves rise as he tilts his head, studying me with amusement. He seems to read every vulnerable emotion I'm wading through, and he lets me sit in the torment. Then, he slides his hand down the door, and his fingertips trail across my stomach.

"Last time you had this on," he says, "you threw me on my ass. I'm hoping you won't do that again once I have you out of these pajamas."

I smile sweetly, cocking my head. "No promises."

Theo snorts, shaking his head, but he slides his hand under my pajamas top. I suck in a breath as his palm slips up my abdomen, my shirt rising with it, and I bite my lip as he cups my breast, squeezing.

"That's a good sign," Theo murmurs as a whimper slips through my lips. His fingers dance across the lace material, finding my nipple, and he grins, giving me a gentle tug.

I melt into the door, shutting my eyes as he pulls and twists. Theo lets out a satisfied sound, and without warning, he gives me a hard pinch.

I gasp, my back arching off the door.

"There's my Red," he murmurs. He stops his slow torture and takes my top off, carefully guiding it over my head. He lets out a long, complimentary whistle as he steps back, taking me in. "You look like the best Christmas present I've ever had."

I roll my eyes, but the flutter in my stomach drops low, everything tightening between my legs. "Then, finish unwrapping me."

Theo's gaze darkens, and he takes a prowling step towards me. He closes the distance between us, my nipples hardening as his chest brushes mine, and he kisses the corner of my mouth. When he drops to one knee, I gasp, and my hand rises, slipping into his hair.

His focus intense, he slides his thumbs into the band of my pants and peels them down, guiding my feet out one by one. He starts to peer up at me, but he does a double take at the scarlet lingerie, eyes zeroing in at what he's just discovered.

"You're not wearing any underwear," he says, his voice guttural with need.

I shake my head, blushing and biting my lip. Theo clears his throat, eyes still locked on my lap where the lace material barely skates over the apex of my thighs, hiding nothing.

"You came into my home, cuddled with me on the couch, and this whole time, you've been wearing that without any underwear."

He arches a brow, and I nod, head spinning because he's so close to me.

Still on his knee, Theo scans me up and down. His tongue sweeps between his lips, and he braces a hand on my hip, tilting me to him. I don't have time to feel too exposed. He guides my legs apart with a nudge of his hand, and then he grips both my hips, holding me still.

Theo's tongue slides over me, parting me, flicking once with a devilish promise.

I shudder, my fingers tightening in his hair while my other palm braces against the door. He moves closer, squeezing my hips, and my knees nearly give out as his mouth closes over my center.

He sucks, and it's like being in the Christmas tree all over again. I have no control over myself, and my hips lift for him, my body craving and needing more.

Theo groans, getting comfortable on the floor, and he slides one hand to my center, the other clutching my hip.

He takes his mouth from me just long enough to study my face as his fingers slide between my legs. He parts me, testing, and when I let out a desperate whimper, he presses in.

My hips buck, and I squeeze my eyes shut as pleasure rocks through me. My head drops back against the door, and Theo thrusts his finger inside again, the heat of his gaze still on me.

"You're so warm," he murmurs. *Thrust, thrust.* He brushes a kiss over my pussy, my clit pulsing with anticipation as his fingers pump into me. "And so wet already."

My fingers twist desperately in his hair, and he obeys my silent plea, opening his mouth and tasting me with his tongue as he pumps and pumps.

"Theo…" I whimper, but he doesn't care that I'm already melting in ecstasy. He adds a second finger, carefully pressing in and moving directly to where I need him. "Oh!"

I cry out, lifting my hips towards him, and he smiles against my skin before he licks me again. His tongue swirls over my center while his fingers circle deep, and he drags the tip of his tongue up, up…

His mouth closes over my clit, and he sucks, and I let out a scream of pleasure. I cup my hand over my mouth, but I'm still gripping his hair, and he knows what I need. He sucks and thrusts, his hand picking up speed, and I shut my eyes, my hand slipping from my mouth and down my chest, taunting my breasts before I can't help it anymore.

I twist both hands into his hair as he starts to devour me, my knees bending, so I slide down the door several inches, giving him better access. He keeps thrusting, keeps sucking, but he spreads me open with that other hand, and I think I might die this Christmas. Little cries of pleasure fly from me, and this man has been living across the street from me for over a year, and he's eating my pussy like it's all he's been dreaming of.

Theo feels me tightening, and he gives me exactly what I need, his fingers pumping fast as his teeth graze over my clit. He sucks and licks and pulls, and I explode, crying out with pleasure.

I can hardly keep myself upright as the waves roll through me, and his fingers keep moving, only slowing when it's clear I need relief. My legs shake, but rather than help me stand, Theo moves back, carefully guiding me to the floor.

There's a massive snowman rug in his entryway, but I hadn't given it much thought before. As I struggle onto my hands and knees, body quaking, I realize how soft it feels, the material nearly spotless. It looks brand new, and as Theo's hands find my hips, I decide it's the perfect place to recover.

Lips press into my asscheek, and I let out a soft sound, smiling at the affectionate gesture. Then, Theo straightens on his knees behind me, and his palm strikes my ass.

I hiss, back arching in surprise as I look over my shoulder at him. I start to glare, but he spanks me again, and my flesh stings.

And it feels good.

So, so good.

A shudder rolls through my body, but I'm not sure I can handle a third slap in the same spot, so I hide my ass by turning and sitting down.

Theo gives me a knowing grin, and I bite my lip because he's coming closer. He moves on his hands and knees, and I drop back on my elbows as he moves over me. His lips are slick with me when he kisses me, and I can't help it. I want him all over again, and I want more.

I cup his face, clinging to him as he lays me down, and he doesn't seem at all concerned for his happy snowman rug. He looks like he has every intention of fucking me right here.

Theo bites my lip, making me gasp, and he lowers himself between my legs. He grinds into me, the soft material of his sweats doing little to hide the hard, unyielding shape of his erection. Every part of me feels so sensitive, and he drags himself against my center, letting me curl my arms around his neck.

"Tell me you want this, Red," he bites out, his voice strained with restraint.

"I want this," I breathe between kisses. "I want you. I want you inside me."

He kisses me again, demonstrating more restraint than I expected, so I drag my hands down his body, finding his sweats. I hook my fingers into the band, trying to tug them down, and he lets out a low chuckle, smiling against my lips. He helps me move his pants down, kicks them off, and he lowers himself, putting his weight on me.

My body cries out with desperation, wanting and needing him because his cock is right against me, resting against my center. I give a little whimper, tilting my hips because I need more. I feel his tip brush against my clit, and I shiver, realizing he's going to take his sweet time.

Theo's elbows are braced on either side of my head, and he sweeps my hair back, studying me. We lock eyes, and he holds my gaze as I finally feel his hips start to pull back. His tip slides down my center, and I suck in a breath, eyes flicking between his because somehow, in this desperate, needy moment, he's made it intimate.

He's staring at me like I'm everything to him, and my mind reels as I try to make sense of when he became so much to me.

Theo presses into me, sinking an inch and I moan, tensing. My legs lift around him, and I grab his shoulders, and I stare at him because oh, my god…

Theo Kase is between my legs, and he knows exactly what he's down. His hips push forward, slowly bringing him deeper, and I'm about to crawl out of my own skin, it feels so good. The remnant waves of my orgasm make me quiver and clench around him, and he smiles as he thrusts home.

And then he's fucking me.

This infuriating, patient, good looking man is fucking me in hard, heavy thrusts that have me clenching around him every time, and he's staring right into my eyes. His palm finds my face and he frames his fingers along my jaw, holding me in place so I can't look away. He sees every bit of pleasure, reading it in my eyes as he moves inside me, thrusting, panting, building.

He's going to make me come again, and he knows it. I'm about to crack and shatter beneath him, and he's ready for it. He pushes his lips to mine, kissing me once, and I tighten, unable to hold out for long.

I break for him, erupting, and his eyes swim over me as sounds of pleasure tear from my throat, his hips moving faster and faster. He draws it out, pulling every last drop of feeling straight to that place between my legs, so I can't even make sense of my own self. I finally shut my eyes because I come so hard, the world starts to blur to the point that I only see him.

Theo grunts — thrusting, thrusting — and he groans, pulling out of me. Something hot melts across my lower abdomen, and I shudder, still riding out the orgasm as his cum coats my tummy where the lingerie has ridden up. My hand drops down automatically, my fingers dipping into where he's marked me, and I lift a drop to my mouth. I press it between my lips, tasting him on my tongue as the orgasm draws to an end, and he groans at the sight of me.

I feel his hand at my hip, and he massages me, eyes studying. Then, he lowers himself next to me, sliding his arm under my head, so he can hold me. He waits until my body stops trembling, giving me soft kisses on my forehead. Then, he kisses my lips and stands to retrieve a towel, murmuring something about taking me upstairs.

TWELVE
THEO

I wake in my bed with Ruby in my arms and her feet tangled between my legs. Something feels so right about waking up like this on Christmas morning. Part of me wants to wake her, but another part of me is scared that if I do, she'll confirm my fears and say last night was a slip in judgement. That she was caught up in the moment of something magical, but the magic faded with the night.

It didn't fade for me.

Her hair is draped across my arm, her head cutting off my circulation, and she looks like the Christmas candy your mom tells you not to touch before breakfast.

Except she's not candy.

She's Ruby. And last night, it felt like she was mine.

I'm not ready to break that spell yet. I like when she looks at me with disdain, but I'm not sure my heart could take that this morning.

I sigh, content to go back to sleep for a few hours, or at least until she wakes up, but just as I close my eyes, my alarm goes off.

I let out a low curse and roll onto my back, reaching for my phone on the nightstand. I shut off the sound, but the damage is done. Ruby rubs her forehead as she squints and blinks the sleep from her eyes. Her nose is wrinkled, and she licks her lips. It takes a moment for her eyes to settle on me. When they do, she freezes.

This is it. This is when she breaks my goddam heart.

"Why are you looking at me like that?" She asks, her voice small, but something about it seems amused. A smile quirks in the corner of her mouth, and she sweeps stray hairs back from her face. "Don't tell me I snore. You look petrified."

My heart doesn't crack, but it feels like it clicks. Or ticks, like the secondhand of a clock. It feels like it's counting down. I'm not quite ready to believe she's happy to wake up here.

Ruby's brows pull together, her green eyes narrowing.

"Theo," she starts, gentler this time. "You're scaring me. You look pale. Is it Santa? Did he explode again?"

This time, I'm not sure whether she's joking or actually concerned.

I let out a small laugh, relieved.

"No," I say, and her expression relaxes as she drops her head onto my arm. Then, the concept of this morning returning to me, I whisper, "Merry Christmas."

I lean forward to kiss her, and she lets me. Not only does she let me, but she cups the side of my face, lifting her head slightly like she doesn't want to stop kissing me.

Her legs shift, tangling further with mine as she starts to move, and I'm wondering whether she fully grasps that I'm me and she's herself and this time yesterday, she hated me.

"Ruby," I start, but she shifts, and it's only natural to move on top of her, bracing my elbows on the bed and framing myself around her. She runs her hands down my naked abdomen, lifting her chin to chase my lips. "Ruby, wait. We should talk about all this."

My words almost get lost as my lips trail her skin, moving along her jaw.

"Talk about what?" she asks, her legs lifting around my hips.

I lower myself, my cock already hard and wanting, but I reach down between us, cupping her. I groan as I feel the slick heat of her.

"You and me," I say, my voice dropping lower than usual. I slide my fingers against her. Then, I press one, desperate finger inside. "This."

Ruby whimpers, her hips lifting, and she turns her face, so her lips are against my ear. "I want this."

Yeah, but for how long?

I don't voice my question. It's Christmas, and she's telling me what she wants, and she's everything I need. I tease her, drawing the pleasure out of her until she's ready, but I can't restrain myself for long.

I press into Ruby Warner on Christmas Day, unable to tear my eyes away from hers. And then I love her desperately because I'm not sure how long this little gift from the universe will last.

Ruby's wearing one of my flannels over her pajamas as she stirs something in a pot in my kitchen. She kept laughing when I asked what she was doing, rummaging through my fridge and pantry. I cleaned up our mess from last night when I realized there was no stopping her, but I've been leaning against the kitchen doorway for at least five minutes, watching her and listening to her talk.

She's cute when she's cooking.

She's downright precious when she smiles and threatens me with the giant, wooden spoon every time I try to get too close.

"Now, you have soup for lunch," she says, pride radiating from her as she turns to look at me. "It'll keep you warm for Christmas, and you'll think of me when you eat it."

The smile that pulls across her lips tugs at my heartstrings, and I step towards her, relieved that she's finally letting me into my own kitchen. I lift a brow at the contents of the pot, mouth water as the medley of scents hits me, and I wrap my arms around her.

"Thank you," I say, planting a kiss on her. "I was going to think of you all day long though. I'm always thinking of you."

Ruby's nose wrinkles, but her eyes are shining with happiness. "That's the sort of thing you should have said sooner. I could have made you soup ten times by now."

We laugh, and she lets me kiss her. I'm not sure if she knows how honest I was being. I'm always thinking of her.

I just had a bad way of showing it.

"I should really get going," she says, but I hear the reluctance in her voice. "I should let you get back to your Christmas plans."

I don't really have plans for today, but I don't want to tell her that. I'm sure she has a million things she wants to do, and given how she felt about me twenty-four hours ago, I doubt she had any intention of being here, in my house, with me.

"I can walk you back," I say, because asking her to stay a bit longer feels like pushing my luck. "I'll go grab your shoes."

I leave Ruby in my kitchen, trying not to think about the future. We don't have to figure it out today. It's Christmas. I'm not going to make her stumble through her mixed-up feelings about me or us. I want more time with her, but I need to let her process everything that has happened. I need to let this breathe.

Ruby's still wearing my flannel over her pajamas when I bring her shoes to her, and I don't ask for it back. She laces herself up, and together, we walk towards her house. As we say goodbye in the road, I can't stop flashes of last night from replaying in my head.

"Have a good Christmas, Ruby Warner," I say. I give her one more kiss — on the cheek, in case she doesn't want the neighbors to ask questions — and watch her disappear inside her house.

THIRTEEN

RUBY

Walking back into my house feels like walking into a sanctuary. So much has happened in less than twenty-four hours, and I'm not even sure how to begin processing things.

First, Santa is real. I killed Santa — temporarily. Then, I saved Christmas with a man I thought I loathed, and now, I'm wondering how that feeling became so blurred that it transformed into something else.

I'm not sure how I feel about Theo Kase.

But I do know that I already wish I was back over there, curled under his arm in front of his TV with the fireplace warming the space.

Last night was… unexpected. It felt different than a hookup. It felt special. He made me feel wanted. But I've known he physically desired me since he saw me in lingerie the first time.

The words he said — last night and this morning — lead me to believe it was more for him than that, but how much more?

When we parted ways, Theo looked like he wanted to say something, and I had a million things I could have said, but none of them felt right. Now, I sense that we're about to get stuck in an awkward limbo that will eventually slip back to where we were before, possibly with less hostility.

I sigh, shrugging out of his flannel that I stupidly wanted to keep because it smells like him. I drop it over the coatrack and take stock of my living room. It looks like the perfect day for Christmas. Usually, I would have a quiet morning before dropping some gifts off to friends. I've tried to stay busy on the holidays without being too intrusive, but my perfectly cozy house feels too quiet.

I go into the kitchen and start up the coffee maker. It's well into the morning, closing in on noon, but it's never too late for caffeine. I stand and watch the pot brew, zoning out until I hear three gentle knocks on my door.

I straighten, caught off guard. I haven't even changed from last night, so I press my hands over the fabric of the pajama set, hoping to calm any wrinkles. I don't look too bad — I just won't look in the mirror. Maybe Jenny or Lindsey decided to drop in on me this year.

When I swing my front door open, the last thing I expect is Theo, but there he is, looking slightly uncomfortable and like he's already regretting the decision to knock on my door.

"I don't mean to interrupt," he says, and he bounces nervously on his feet with his hands behind his back. "I know we just said goodbye a few minutes ago, but I was wondering if I could come in."

"Sure," I say, surprised. I back away, making room for him. As he steps inside, I catch a glimpse of what he's holding behind his back. There's a small box wrapped in red in his hands, complete with a vibrant green ribbon. "You got me a present?"

Theo's head snaps towards me, his eyes widening. Then, he smiles and drops his gaze to the floor, bringing his hands forward.

"I did," he admits, shaking his head. His eyes flick to mine, searching. "I was going to give it to you last night after the festival, but then Santa happened, and… well."

He shrugs and extends the package to me.

"I didn't get you anything," I say, feeling a little guilty.

He'd bought me a present before last night? He had this already?

"That's okay," he says, and he closes my front door. "I've had it for a while. I thought about not giving it to you, but I figured, why not?"

I bite my lip, smiling at the gesture.

"Thank you," I say, tugging at the ribbon. It falls away easily, and I carefully unwrap the gleaming paper. "Really, you didn't have to get me something. Now, we feel unbalanced."

Theo watches my hands, falling silent as I open the box.

There's some tissue paper cushioning the inside, so I remove it and freeze.

It's a snow globe.

I peek at him, a small grin on my face.

"You know I love Christmas," I say, feeling that new, rare appreciation for him. "Thank you."

"You should pull it out of the box," he says, nodding towards the unseen globe.

Oh no...

I frown, then carefully pull it free, and...

Oh.

"Oh."

Theo chuckles, stepping closer as I stare at the thing.

"It winds up," he says, and I can hear the amusement in his voice.

"Oh, you don't have to..."

But he does. Theo finds the metal piece, twists it, and gives the snow globe a little shake. Music starts to play and fake, sparkly snow swirls around, and in the center, the figurines start to turn.

"Why?" I groan, giving him a pleading look. "I have to hide this up in my room or something. It can't go in the living room."

He shrugs again. "At least you'll see it and think of me before you go to bed."

I roll my eyes and glare at him, but I can't quite keep the smile from my lips.

"This is despicable," I say, holding it up for him to see.

"It was custom made," he says, his smile stretching across his face.

I sigh and take in the globe again, trying to appreciate it.

Just like the decorations in his yard, there's a pole-dancing reindeer spinning in the center of the snow globe. Except, it's not just a reindeer. There's a red-headed woman in scarlet lingerie swinging around the opposite side, white trim detailing her outfit to make her look more seasonal.

"Why does she look like me?" I ask, sounding fed up.

"I told you," he laughs, stepping towards me. "I had it custom made. I thought you'd forgive me for the lingerie scandal if I gave you a memento."

I groan, dropping my head back, but Theo takes the globe from me and sets it on a table. Then, he plants his hands on my hips, staring at me until I lift my head and meet his gaze.

"Ruby… Ms. Warner…" he trails off, clearing his throat when I lift a quizzical brow. When I don't interrupt, he continues, "I just had one question for you."

I cock my head to the side in challenge, staring him down. "And what is that, Mr. Kase?"

Theo grins, liking the challenge. "What are you doing for New Years Eve, Red?"

FOURTEEN

THEO

The town is buzzing with anticipation, and the parks are filled with snow.

I walk around the bottom of Firefly Hill, remembering how I nearly rocketed into the parking lot almost a week ago. If it hadn't been for Ruby, I'm not sure I would have made it to Christmas.

My mom and sister are already at the top of the hill, holding down the place we'd picked out with blankets over their shoulders and coco in their hands. They're waiting to see the fireworks as soon as the clocks strike midnight, but what they don't know is they're about to meet the woman that's lived rent-free in my head since I moved here.

I see the front of her familiar truck first, and my eyes drift as I hear the driver's door close. Ruby steps around the side, coming onto the sidewalk just as I close in to meet her.

"Hey," she says, face lighting with surprise. I hadn't told her I was coming down to the parking lot. "I was about to text you if I couldn't find you."

I smile and bend to kiss her, soaking in the way she puts her hands on my waist. She always seems like she's bracing herself and melting into me at the same time, and I cup the back of her head, prolonging the kiss.

"My mom and sister are in rare form," I warn her, and her eyes widen with concern. "I'm pretty sure there's booze in their hot chocolate, and they're both decked out in silver tassels."

Slowly, Ruby grins. "Perfect."

"I also didn't tell them you were coming," I say, wanting to get the admission out of the way.

Her face falls with disappointment.

"They would have had a matching outfit for you," I say, grimacing.

Her disappointment steadies out, turning to understanding, and she rises onto her toes to kiss me one more time. "Tassels aren't the *worst* thing in the world."

We make our way to the top of Firefly Hill, weaving through families and couples spread out on picnic blankets. For a moment, I think I've lost where I've left my family, but then silver clashes with pink, and two very similar and familiar faces turn towards me.

"Oh, you jerk!" My sister, Suzy, calls. "You should have told us she was coming! I knew you had a secret!"

My mom gives me a mildly disapproving glare, but she shakes her head, a grin forming. Then, she turns her attention to Ruby. "Are you the girl that's kept my Theo on his toes all year?"

I feel the moment Ruby hesitates. She doesn't know what I've told my family about her. She doesn't know that the affectionate and admiring stories started well before the events on Christmas Eve.

Ruby steals a glance at me, and I cringe, feeling exposed.

"I told them about the cookies you brought over," I admit, realizing I'm going to reveal a bit of the timeline. "Not the Christmas Eve cookies, but the first ones. And I told them how you walk Mrs. Barry's cats."

Ruby's gaze softens, but I watch as she steels herself, not giving away too much. She smiles at my mom and sister, shrugging. "He's easy to be around."

Relief sweeps through me, but then my mom laughs.

"Well, that's very polite of you, but I know my son." She opens her arms and embraces Ruby, giving me a sharp look. "I hope whatever attitude he gives you, you serve it right back. He had to put up that armor he wears to keep up with us girls. I'm afraid he felt outnumbered most of his childhood."

"Mom," I groan, but Suzy pipes in, starting some story about one of the times they bedazzled the living room, eager to share my various forms of rebellion.

Ruby laughs. "Okay, so getting under someone's skin is a skill he's been building all his life."

My mom and sister laugh, throwing their heads back.

"I like her," Suzy murmurs, nudging me in the ribs. "Good job, bro."

Around us, people start counting down. From sixty.

"A whole minute?" Suzy asks, scrunching her nose.

"The town is very enthusiastic about the holidays," Ruby explains, nodding solemnly.

I loop my arm around her, joining in the countdown as my mom and sister force sparkle-covered kazoos into our hands. The town counts down, the clock strikes midnight, and noise erupts around us.

But I'm not blowing my kazoo.

No, I'm looking right at Ruby, and she looks right at me. I brush her hair back, the world blurring around her because she's all I see. I bring my mouth to hers, and I kiss her the same way I've kissed her every day since Christmas Eve.

"Aw, gross," Suzy coos. "My brother has a girlfriend."

She bumps into me from behind, making me stumble into Ruby, so I glare at her over my shoulder.

"We wore matching outfits for Christmas Eve," Ruby pipes in, surprising me. I turn to look at her, and she smiles guiltily, shrugging. "Red velvet, white trim… Total Santa vibes."

Suzy laughs, and my mom's mouth drops open in surprise.

"He still has it in his closet," Ruby says, ignoring me as I pinch her hip in warning. "It was for the winter festival. I'm going to make him wear it again next year."

There it is. The thing I've been needing to hear.

Suddenly, putting on matching Santa costumes for my mom and sister's amusement doesn't sound so bad.

"Next year, huh?" I ask, tugging her against me.

She smirks at me, her eyes flashing with amusement.

"Do you have a problem with that?"

She's daring me to mess with her. She's dangling temptation right in front of me."

"Not at all, Red."

Her cheeks heat, and her eyes widen with warning.

"Red?" Suzy asks. "Now, that's a cliché nickname."

"Well," I say, enjoying Ruby's panic and glaring a little too much even though I have no intention of really explaining. "There's a bit of a funny story…"

Ruby bends down and scoops up the snow. Before I have time to comprehend what she's doing, she clumps it into a ball and throws it. It hits me right in the face.

"Oh, Red," I laugh, wiping the freezing mess from my face. I glare at her as I stoop to the ground. "You're going down."

Ruby takes off running, and my sister trails her, laughing. My mom's smart enough to grab her tarp-lined picnic blanket and wrap it around herself, making a dash for the parking lot. The world erupts — snow flying, people laughing — and I chase down Ruby Warner, realizing our fun is just beginning.

Ruby Warner and I have been at war since I moved in across the street. It just took us a while to realize we didn't always have to be on opposing teams.

ONE YEAR LATER
RUBY

"Another peppermint!" I shout, turning around to grab the next cup. The winter festival is in full swing, and the hot chocolate has brought everyone together.

"This one's classic — for Ms. B." Theo presses the Styrofoam cup into my hand, grinning before he turns back around.

We have a lot of helpers, and his pies are steaming and fresh. The world feels like a whirlwind, but I keep passing and pouring and taking orders. We combined our setup this year, and something about it feels just right. Jenny and Lindsey aren't looking at me with sympathy like they usually do. Actually, they look a little envious as their eyes flick between me and Theo.

"Here's that peppermint," he says, his voice a deep murmur in my ear. I feel his hand press into my lower back as he brings the cup around me. I take it and rise onto my toes, letting him kiss my cheek.

"Thanks!"

His mom and sister helped decorate his house this year, and their dedication to making things extra girly makes me understand Theo's preference for slightly inappropriate decor. They even lined my porch with furry, pink snowflakes that light up in sync to music, and they're visiting through New Years. Theo warned me that their Christmas decorating has nothing on the party they're going to help us throw for New Years Eve. I'm both intrigued and terrified.

As the night goes on, so many people drop by to wish us happy holidays. Some of them share anecdotes about my aunt and uncle, but something happens this year that hasn't happened before. Several people tell me they would have been proud of me. It's a bittersweet sentiment that has my eyes stinging all night, but being surrounded by loved ones makes it easier to appreciate.

Not that Theo is a loved one. We haven't made it that far.

But Jenny and Lindsey are there, unaware of the disaster that happened after the festival last year. I'm sure they would have my head examined if I told them Santa was real, so I've let them live with their curiosity about how Theo and I made amends.

The less they know, the better.

Actually, the less anyone knows about that night, the better.

After Jamison moved to take on a big promotion in a nearby city, Lindsey bought his house, so I've had both of them keeping a close eye on me. I'll just let them think what they want.

When we pack up, there's no hot chocolate left. Theo sends off the extra supplies with Timmy, who still works at Dish & Dally. Then, we climb into my truck, Theo taking the driver's seat since he finally won me over a few months ago, and he steers us towards home.

We're barely out of the truck when we see something strange.

"What's that?" I ask, pointing at the roof of his house.

"No," Theo says, dread clear in his voice. "It can't be."

"That's definitely him!" I burst, eyes widening with shock. "But we're getting along! What's he doing here?"

Theo starts moving across the street, and I follow close on his heels. He scans his yard, then his windows, but he visibly relaxes when there's no sign of his mom or sister's return.

"What are you doing up there?" Theo shouts, not even giving me a chance to plan.

Santa yelps, waving his arms wildly like he's about to lose his balance again.

No, no — not again!

He catches himself, grabbing the chimney.

"Oh, hi you two!" he laughs, resting his hand on his stomach, just above his belt. "Just wanted to check in on my two favorite troublemakers. Both of you made the nice list!"

I blink, dumbfounded, but Theo isn't letting the possible disasters strike tonight.

"No offense, Santa," he calls, "but we were kind of

hoping we wouldn't see you this year. Or ever."

Santa's laugh is long and rolling and full of cheer. "Oh, you two. You're both so funny. See, this is why I came to visit! I thought I'd start my night off right! And the reindeer are having a snack. The flowers in your backyard are the only things not frozen over, Theo!"

"Great," Theo mutters. He shoves his hands in his pocket, finally turning to me for help.

I shrug, not sure what to do either.

Up on the roof, Santa casts a look in the backyard. Then, he whirls towards us, frowning. "You didn't happen to have any pine cones in your backyard, did you, Theo? George, the one flying front and center this year, gets a little interesting if he finds some pine cones."

Theo gapes at him, shrugging. "I mean, there's a few pine cones, yeah."

"Uh oh." Santa turns, staring at the back yard. "No, George! Don't eat that!"

There's a jingle and a horrible crashing sound. Then, there's the undeniable shape of deer cutting across the sky, moving so fast, a few of them are just a blur.

"Oh dear," Santa says, shaking his head. He turns and looks down at us. "I suppose I need your help again. The harnesses must have been old, and George spooked them all. He's the only one left down there, munching away."

I cringe and Theo groans.

"How are we supposed to help with the reindeer?" Theo snaps, waving his pocketed hands in frustration.

Santa gets a strange look on his face, and he grins. "If I

remember correctly, you are quite the horseback rider, Theo."

"Great," Theo mutters, and as he turns to look at me, Santa starts rummaging in his pockets. He finds a piece of paper and folds it before sending it down as a paper airplane.

"This should help you on your journey!" Santa says, rubbing his stomach and smiling. "I'm just going to shimmy down your chimney for a snack. George should be fine in the yard. Try not to take too long!"

There's a pop and a crack, and Santa leaps into the air. Before our eyes, he shrinks down to the size of a large raccoon, landing atop the chimney.

"He can't be serious," Theo mutters, watching him slide away. "All those cookies you made are in there."

"Then I guess we better hurry," I say, unfolding the paper airplane. It's a map, just as before. But this time, eight glowing reindeer shapes fly across the page. "At least we can see where they all are. And it looks like you don't have to touch the map at the same time. We can split up and go faster!"

"Ruby, I'm not letting you wrangle a reindeer on your own," Theo says, shutting down the conversation.

Two sets of headlights turn onto the street, coming from opposite directions. We wait, watching as his mom and sister pull into his driveway next to us. In Lindsey's driveway next door, Jenny and Lindsey hop out, waving at us.

"You thinking what I'm thinking?" Theo asks, lifting a

brow.

"We don't need to involve them," I warn. There are a million things that could go wrong.

Theo ignores me, a smile growing on his face.

"Hey mom!" He calls, walking towards her car. "There's someone inside I want you to meet. He needs our help."

Theo approaches his family, not waiting for my approval. I sigh, looking over my shoulder at my friends who are staring curiously. Resigned, I wave them over.

"It's Christmas, after all," I say to myself. "It's supposed to be about coming together."

Jenny and Lindsey hurry over as they realize I'm approaching.

Then, together, we all turn and walk towards Theo's house.

"Everyone," Theo says, and he gives me a final look.

I shrug, feeling nervous, but deciding to say it together. "Santa needs our help."

A NOTE FROM VICKI SWEETS

Hello readers! Thank you so much for reading *Christmas Is Doomed!* This book was such a delight to write, and the experience was made so much sweeter by the support and excitement coming from those I've connected with over the years in the writing and reading community.

I wish you all happy holidays, and I look forward to connecting with you next year! You can find me on various social media platforms, and you may check for the latest book updates on my website:

www.vickisweets.com

If you would like to make sure you hear about new book releases, please follow my Amazon Author Page, Goodreads, or Instagram.